The Girl on the Doorstep

A Berkshires Cozy Mystery

Andrea Kress

The Girl on the Doorstep

A Berkshires Cozy Mystery

Andrea Kress

Table of Contents

Chapter 1

Defying the laws of probability, there has been another tragic death at Highfields. And such a short time after the last one.

But what, you may ask, am I, Aggie Burnside, still doing in West Adams, Massachusetts? I was supposed to start my job as a registered nurse in June in the New York City hospital where I trained, but the woman whom I was to replace stayed on while her fiancé recovered from German measles. Lucky for them, he did. They got married and then he lost his job, not an unusual thing in the Great Depression, so she stayed on at the hospital.

Unlucky for me. But in the meantime, what began as a temporary, half-time appointment for me in West Adams assisting Dr. John Taylor became more or less permanent. I may not have made as much money as in New York, but the benefits were numerous.

One of them was John Taylor, but more about him later.

Another advantage was I got to be on my own for the first time in my young life in a warm and interesting household. I had possession of a spacious, sunny bedroom rented from Miss Manley, an elderly spinster whose maid, Annie, provided excellent meals as well as laundry services. I had my friend Glenda's car at my disposal and Miss Manley herself was a treat—an engaging conversationalist entirely involved in the goings-on and gossip of West Adams through her wide circle of friends. It was a change for me, having grown up in the more suburban Pelham, New York, where neighbors tended to keep a polite distance, whereas in West Adams doors were left unlocked, people popped in unannounced and any new tidbit of information spread miraculously by word of mouth, across a fence, on the street or by telephone in record time.

We first learned of the death from Elsie, Reverend Lewis's maid, who scurried across the yard from through the back door into our kitchen to give the news to Annie as Miss Manley and I were coming down to breakfast. Passing the open door, I glanced in, and I greeted the two maids.

They stopped their whispering and opened eyes wide at me.

"Whatever is the matter?" Miss Manley asked.

The phone rang and Annie answered, handing the earpiece to me, still gaping.

It was Dr. Taylor.

"There's been a death at Highfields," he said.

"I know," I said.

He gave me a few more details in his usual concise manner as I listened, wordlessly.

"Come over and I'll drive you up with me," he added.

I replaced the earpiece and turned to Miss Manley with the two maids close behind.

"There's been a death at Highfields," I repeated.

Miss Manley clutched the cameo at the neck of her blouse, the blue veins standing out on the back of her hand.

"Not Christa?" she asked.

I tend to be calm in times of crisis or emotion, and I think my lack of reaction initially unnerved all three women.

"No, not Christa. Dr. Taylor said there was the body of a girl on the doorstep."

Chapter 2

Let me back up a bit to explain some of the changes in West Adams since I first arrived earlier in the summer. The former residents of Highfields had left for Boston, leaving behind a furnished house to be rented out for an indeterminate amount of time. I was pleased that the previously planned, stark Art Deco renovations hadn't been done and the home was left as its stately old-fashioned self. Not that it was any of my business. Some of the servants were kept on to maintain the house in proper order and that seemed to suit the new tenants, the Broadway producer Montgomery Davis and his actress wife Christa Champion.

It was rather exciting to have such well-known visitors to our little town although I had seen them only once driving toward me on Main Street when I took a break to go to the post office. Christa was recognizable from the face I had seen as a teenager on huge posters that hung at the train station in Pelham when I took the train into Manhattan. When I was growing up, she was featured as the star in many musicals, with reviews and advertisements in the theater section of the newspapers. Since the Depression began, however, some theaters had closed, and I wondered if that was why she and her husband were able to take a vacation. I hoped she hadn't retired because I should have liked to see her on stage.

In fact, I had only been to one Broadway musical—on my eighteenth birthday with my parents. I was completely overwhelmed by the spectacle of the excitement of the crowd waiting to go in, the seemingly small stage so far away, the seats crammed close together with hardly any legroom for a tall girl such as myself. But once the orchestra struck up the overture, everyone was silent in anticipation until the last flourish of the conductor, when the curtains opened and the first words of dialogue put the play into motion.

Later, when I lived in the City during my nurses' training, I assumed I would be taking in plays and musicals regularly. Alas, my medical student dates were as short on cash as I was, and movies were the affordable substitute. I planned to be back home for a visit at Thanksgiving, and just seeing Christa Champion disappearing down the street made me vow that I would see a Broadway show in November, come what may.

Some days before the incident at Highfields, I was at work at my usual half-day afternoon shift at Dr. Taylor's office, assembling bills to be paid and preparing the invoices to be sent out to the patients. I was pleased to note that the income of the practice had increased noticeably in the short time since I first arrived, not only because there were more patients but also due to timely billing and collection, which I admitted proudly was my doing.

The phone rang in the reception room and almost before I could say hello, a man's panicked voice said his boss was experiencing chest pains and could the doctor see him right away.

"Who is the patient?" I asked, but it sounded as if he had dropped the telephone's handset because I could hear people talking. I pressed the call button several times, but someone had hung up.

The doctor, reading one of his medical journals in his office behind me, called out.

"Aggie, who was that?"

"I don't know. He didn't say."

He shrugged and, although I was puzzled, we resumed our respective tasks.

Not more than five minutes later, we heard a car screech to a halt on the street outside, followed by feet pounding on the pavement and then the door was flung open by a red-faced man who looked at me and then the doctor at the desk facing the door in the room behind me.

"Sir, are you all right?" I asked, hoping he was not the man with the chest pains who had run to our door.

"No, in the car! CR!"

He turned and ran back the way he had come with the two of us trotting to keep up. He led us to a large, black car with a grey-faced man in the passenger seat.

The doctor flung the door open, partially unbuttoned the man's shirt, loosened the man's tie, all while questioning him about how he felt. I stood to the side next to the panting younger man who had led us there.

"Whatever I felt seems to be passing," the man in the car said.

"Are you able to walk into my office?" the doctor asked.

With the young man on one side and the doctor on the other, they escorted the heavyset man slowly up the walkway while I left the door open and then scurried to the examining room to make sure it was ready.

His face seemed to have regained color, possibly just from the action of walking, but he sat down heavily on the exam table and pulled his tie off completely.

"That was really something," he said and tried a weak smile. "Bernard, you can wait outside," he added, gesturing vaguely with his hand.

"Would you like me to stay?" I asked, and the doctor shook his head.

I closed the door to the examining room and approached the man who stood before me with fear in his eyes while he struggled to put his hair in place with his fingers.

"Thank you for bringing him in," I said. "Would you like a glass of water?"

He nodded and sat down in one of the waiting room chairs while I made my way into the doctor's house through a door to his kitchen and returned shortly thereafter. He gulped down half the glass and exhaled loudly.

"I'm Bernard Symington," he said, extending his hand as I introduced myself. "We were driving through town on our way back to the Mountain Aire Hotel and CR gave out a loud groan and suddenly looked awful. I stopped the car immediately and all he said was 'drug store,' pointing to the one on Main Street. I ran in and realized I didn't know why I was in there but seeing the telephone asked the pharmacist to dial the nearest doctor's number. I'm sorry I was so abrupt and vague, but, my God, I was scared."

I sat down next to him. "CR?"

"Cash Ridley. My boss. I stopped talking and asked someone where your office was. Thank God it was so near."

"Yes, that was quick thinking on your part. Had he been doing anything strenuous just before that incident?"

"No. I was driving us back to the hotel after a rather large lunch and he was quieter than usual in the car. I thought perhaps he ate too much or was tired. And then that groan." He swept his free hand across his wide brow and patted his hair into place.

"Don't worry. The doctor will do his best."

I got up and returned to the desk to resume the billing, looking up from time to time to judge how Bernard was doing, pleased to see he was calming down. I glanced at my watch to see that fifteen minutes had gone by without much conversational murmuring coming from the door behind me. Another few minutes and the doctor emerged, drying his hands on a towel.

"How is he?" Bernard asked, standing up.

"Better, much better. He believes he may have had a mild heart attack, but I'm not so sure. Sometimes indigestion can mimic the symptoms of angina and vice versa. He said that he does not have heart problems, do you know if that's true? I only ask because sometimes men don't like to admit there is a physical problem, even to a physician."

"I've been his assistant for almost four years, and I've never seen him like that."

"He said you were staying at the Mountain Aire Hotel, on the way to Pittsfield?"

Bernard nodded.

"I gave him some medicine just now that should stabilize him and more for later. Every eight hours as needed." Dr. Taylor placed the small envelope of pills in the assistant's hand. "Can you call me this evening and let me know how he is doing? And in the morning as well? I can certainly come over to check on him tomorrow if that is suitable."

"Yes, I know he would like that."

We managed to get Mr. Ridley up and out to the car although he seemed to be walking well, if deliberately, on his own. He turned when they reached the car and said to the doctor, "How much do I owe you?" He looked to Bernard, who evidently handled such things.

To my knowledge, that was a first in my experience of this small town, where people came to be treated and waited to be billed later, and the doctor was taken aback.

"I'll be over to see you tomorrow. We'll talk then. Please, take care."

I checked my watch as we went back in, anxious to get back to Miss Manley's weekly tea group where the latest town news was discussed, dissected and dispersed.

"Aggie?"

"Yes, John?"

Since we were alone, we had gotten into the habit of informality at the end of the day.

"Off to hear the latest social infractions of the town?" he asked, smiling as he leaned against the doorway of his office, referring to Miss Manley's tea group. Then his face became serious.

"An interesting thing happened earlier today. Dr. Mitchell dropped in on me, and I expected he was going to ask how things were going in general or follow up with particular patients." He sat on the corner of the reception desk.

He had been filling in for Dr. Mitchell in the mornings in Adams while I assisted only in the afternoons at John's practice in West Adams.

"But his news was startling. Evidently, he has been ex-perienceing heart problems—something he never confided in me although I always thought his color could be better. This vacation of his was at the insistence of his wife and the long and short of it is he wishes to relinquish his practice."

"What does it mean for you?" I asked.

"Mitch has always been a generous person, but this is beyond my expectations. He is going to give it to me with all his patients." He looked surprised as he said it.

"Would you continue to split your days between here and Adams?" I asked.

"I have just begun to think about how I would manage it. On the one hand, I don't want to maintain two offices, and when winter comes, I would prefer not to be traveling these winding, icy roads each day. On the other hand, if I have one office, I would need to decide which location to choose. Dr. Mitchell has a more established practice, of course, having been here so much longer and he has more patients than I, so it would make sense to relocate there. But I wouldn't want the townspeople here to think I am abandoning them by moving my office."

"Is it so far to go to make a difference for patients in either town?" I asked.

"Just a few miles. But you see how many patients are not only walk-ins, but they also actually walk here."

He looked at me intently while he mulled the conundrum.

"I suppose the nature of medicine is changing," I commented. "People can't expect to live in small towns and have all the facilities at their disposal. I'm sure you'll think of a solution."

"How about this: why don't you come over to Mitchell's office tomorrow morning with me and tell me what you think. Perhaps I am too close to the problem to see a solution."

"I'd be glad to," I said, not having seen much of the town of Adams.

"Good," he said, slapping both thighs as he got up.

"Well, duty calls." I said, smiling at him. I took the sweater from the back of the chair and walked the short distance across his back garden to the edge of Reverend Lewis's property, and then left into Miss Manley's back garden. I could see through the French windows that the tea party was in full swing with some dining room chairs backed up to the glass, so I went toward the kitchen door, only to be called back by Mrs. Lewis.

"Aggie! Wait!"

Nina hustled across the grass as quickly as possible in a dress with a slim skirt that inhibited her progress.

"I'm late as usual. You can be my cover or distraction or whatever it is to deflect any attention from my bad manners."

"Nonsense," I said admiring her outfit of lilac-colored cotton. "May I inquire if you got that frock from the Misses Smith?" I asked, referring to the sisters who owned the dress shop and women's alterations business on Main Street.

She giggled. "Of course not! It's from my last foray into Pittsfield. Miss Smith the Elder spotted me when I walked past today and shot me an icy stare. Now, if I knew how to sew, she might think that I made it myself. Unfortunately, the cat was out of the bag when she saw my handiwork on an altar cloth last year."

Miss Manley's kitchen was empty since it was Annie's afternoon off, a well-deserved respite after having baked the several cakes that the ladies in the next room were taking with their tea. She had thoughtfully left a small plate of petit fours on the enamel-topped kitchen table in the event I came back late from work. Life was good.

The conversation muted as Nina and I entered the parlor, then picked up in volume as we were both met with up-and-down glances at our attire: me in my nurse's uniform and the reverend's wife in her lilac-colored confection. By the strained looks in her direction, I could tell that most of the women in the room thought a minister's wife should be wearing something more sedate, less stylish, and certainly not as form-fitting. In contrast, my starched white, mid-calf- length uniform and distinctive cap indicated I was a serious working girl and that met with their approval.

Greetings were made all around to the familiar women who were the backbone of the community—judgmental perhaps, but in a pinch, willing to step in and help anyone who needed assistance.

Miss Manley gestured to two empty chairs for us and poured tea while commenting, "We were just talking about the interesting new neighbors at Highfields."

I overheard Miss Olsen murmur, "Hardly neighbors."

I didn't know if she meant because Highfields was not in the town proper but up the hill, or if people who could afford such a luxurious house were not likely to be neighborly. That was certainly the case with the last inhabitants.

Mrs. Proctor said, "They are *show people*, did you know?" to the assembled group who clucked in disapproval. "Broadway!" she said in a slightly horrified tone.

"Their names are Montgomery Davis and Christa Champion," Miss Manley said.

Looks were exchanged indicating their names alone spoke of show business, a somewhat tawdry profession.

"I saw them driving through town," I offered.

Heads swiveled in my direction.

"I recognized Christa Champion from photos I saw in the newspapers in New York City," I said.

"What in the world are they doing here?" Miss Tierney asked at the roomful of heads, shaking.

It seemed perfectly obvious to me what they were doing in West Adams. "Taking a vacation from the stifling heat in the City, I imagine," I said, taking a bite of a petit four.

While the women in that room had an impression of New York City as a den of iniquity, a place of unimaginable wealth and privilege, the notion that West Adams had something more desirable, even if it was only the weather, had come as a pleasant shock. They waited for more information on that front.

"The City has so many high-rise buildings and skyscrapers that whatever breeze you might expect from the Atlantic Ocean or the Hudson River is only felt if you live next to the water. And of course, there are miles of cement sidewalks that hold the heat."

Nods all around, and suddenly it made sense.

"All right," said Miss Ballantine, "I can understand wanting to escape from the heat but why West Adams?"

"Indeed!" someone said.

"And why not?" the reverend's wife said. "Such a lovely town and the scenic beauties of the Berkshires. Who could ask for more?"

She was back in their good graces.

"But why in the world do *theater people* have such preposterous names? Christa Champion. Really!" Mrs. Myers closed her eyes momentarily as if affronted.

"Actually, I went to school with Christa's mother. And the family name actually is Champion."

The room was quiet for a moment. Imagine! Miss Manley knew theater people.

"I met her years ago when she was a young girl. Charming young thing. I understand she has had a very successful career in musical theater. Her husband has done very well for himself producing plays, too."

By the looks on the faces of the assembled group, it was clear they didn't know what a producer did, but then, neither did I exactly. A bit embarrassed by our collective ignorance, the topic changed.

"What a coincidence. Did you know that Glenda's tenant is a playwright?" Nina asked.

Glenda was my classmate from nurse's training who owned the house next door to Miss Manley, had married her nephew, Stuart Manley, and since they now resided in New York City, she rented out her house. She would have enjoyed this conversation immensely.

"I'm surprised he has any time to write with all the parties and house guests he has," Mrs. Myers said with a sniff of disapproval.

"His name is Douglas something-or-other. I hadn't noticed the parties," I said truthfully.

"I believe your room faces the back and the woods. It's probably why you haven't heard all the ruckus. Since we're across the street and down a few, we can see and hear all kinds of comings and goings." To clarify, she said, "Young women and men. Lots of automobiles. Parties."

I thought it odd Miss Manley hadn't mentioned any noise since her bedroom faced the street, and I exchanged looks with Nina, wondering if she had noticed anything. She shook her head.

"And the place is starting to look a shambles," Mrs. Proctor said, pursing her lips. "Doesn't take his mail in for days, hasn't mowed the lawn...."

"Probably doesn't know how," someone murmured.

"Can't be bothered to deadhead the golden climber," Mrs. Proctor continued. "Yard is littered with blossoms."

"Dear Sarah loved that rose bush so," Miss Manley said wistfully, referring to Glenda's mother.

"Speaking of wild goings-on," Mrs. Rockmore said, "I heard that the Mountain Aire Hotel, which used to be such a respectable place, is now hosting a lot of City people." By which she meant New Yorkers. "And where they used to have a sedate dining room, they now have live entertainment." She was pleased to be the only one present who knew of it.

In response to the surprised looks of the women in the room, she added, "The Fosters have recently put a lot of money into it, advertising in New York newspapers, even. My nephew, Fred, has been working there this summer. Quite a nice job as a bellboy, with a uniform, meals and a view of the entertainment from the wings, as he says."

She said made it sound like a burlesque show took place each night. This might be something John and I would have to check out and I decided to accompany him on his house call to the hotel tomorrow.

As the talk veered into the more mundane, but no less engaging, topic of backyard tomato production, I hoped to leave the party to change out of my uniform and put my feet up for a while. To my immense relief, the telephone rang and, knowing Annie was not there to answer it, I nodded at Miss Manley and retreated to the kitchen where the instrument hung on the wall next to the hallway. I pushed the door shut behind me and pulled a kitchen chair close.

"Hello?" The line crackled a bit.

"Aggie! Hello, it's Glenda."

"Is everything all right?" I asked. Long-distance calls were costly and therefore rare, made usually only in cases of emergency.

"I'm fine. I'm at Stuart's office waiting for him to be done with some editorial meeting and I got bored. So, I thought I would call you."

"Won't he be angry to know you're making telephone calls?"

"They won't know until the bill comes in next month and they won't be able to remember who made the call." She giggled.

That was Glenda. Living for the moment and dealing with the consequences later if anyone noticed.

"Tell me what's going on," she said.

"It's tea party day so the gossip is going hot and heavy in the next room. Theater people are living at Highfields, your renter is ruffling feathers with his loud parties and visitors, nothing too exciting."

"And Doctor Taylor?" she asked in a knowing voice.

"He is well. I'll tell him you asked."

"Come on, Aggie. That's not what I meant," she persisted.

"Very busy with his practice. Oh, I forgot to tell you that the Mountain Aire Hotel now has live entertainment of some kind. We're going there tomorrow to see a patient but I'm awfully curious about what's going on. You remember when we ate there with Stuart and Miss Manley that it was kind of a staid establishment."

"Do they have dancing girls?" Glenda joked.

"Who knows?"

"That settles it. Stuart and I are coming up this weekend and I intend to see what all the fuss is about."

"I don't think it would be correct for a young pregnant woman to be cavorting about in a nightclub," I teased.

"I am hardly showing, the morning sickness is over, and you can't call Mountain Aire a nightclub if they don't serve alcohol."

"Which you shouldn't be drinking now anyway," I said.

"Since Miss Manley is busy with her guests just now, could you let her know that we'll be up Friday evening?"

I thought it more appropriate that her husband ask his aunt directly for them to spend the weekend, but again, that was Glenda.

"Will do. Oh, and can you bring up some Danish pastries?"

"Anything else?" I detected a note of sarcasm.

"A bottle of gin would be perfect. I haven't had a decent martini in a very long time."

She sighed. "I suppose I need to bring vermouth and olives as well."

"Perfect! I'll make some hors d'oeuvres."

"You mean Annie will. Do you know, I've been thinking that since Stuart and I had a courthouse wedding we missed out on a wedding reception."

She was fishing but I didn't bite.

"Maybe we could plan a little party?" she asked.

"Certainly not for this weekend?" There wasn't enough time, and I wasn't keen on being tasked with the job.

"Oh, there's Stuart now. Got to go!" Glenda hung up abruptly.

I laughed and replaced the earpiece onto the cradle of the old-fashioned phone. I was looking forward to seeing Glenda despite her disingenuous treatment of me in the past and the resulting difficult departure not so long ago. I would just have to pretend it hadn't happened, although it was obvious it was long in the past as far as she was concerned.

It could be a fun weekend as long as we didn't have to deal with Stuart, who John thought was a 'gas bag' as he put it, but we might be able to take in the entertainment at the Mountain Aire with them, which wouldn't involve much conversation. What could go wrong, I thought, as I popped another petit four into my mouth.

Chapter 3

I changed out of my uniform and lay on the chenille bedspread, knowing after stuffing myself with all those sweets earlier I could not possibly eat any of the cold dinner that Annie had left for us. One of the windows overlooking the back garden was open and the breeze blew the sheer curtains in and out softly. A few breaths later and I was asleep.

A discreet knock on the door woke me and I pulled on my bathrobe while getting up.

Miss Manley stood outside in the hall apologetically.

"I wonder if you could help me with the tea things," she asked.

"I'm sorry, of course! You shouldn't do them on your own. I just put my feet up and my head down...."

There were large trays in the kitchen and between us we managed to pick up the plates, cups, saucers and utensils in two trips and put them into the hot sudsy water in the sink.

"I'll wash," I said, beginning the familiar job of washing and rinsing and putting the wet items onto the wooden drainboard. Miss Manley took a towel and began the drying process. I remember once asking my mother why we didn't just let plates air dry and her horrified look in return told me that it simply wasn't done. The implication was that perhaps slovenly people did that, but not our family.

"I am sorry my friends have such a disapproving view of Christa and her husband," Miss Manley said.

"I agree. Why do people jump to conclusions?"

"Of course, I don't know her husband at all, and it has been years since I've seen Christa, but I'm sure she can't have changed that much. Her mother was always rather nice."

I turned to face her. "Why don't you invite her to tea with the other ladies and it might open their eyes."

Miss Manley tilted her head to the side and smiled. "What a good idea. But you know, I think I will take it upon myself to call on her first in the event she doesn't remember who I am."

"Very wise. And you will be able to see for yourself whether she can leave her feather boa aside and put on something dowdy to have tea with the gals."

Miss Manley laughed. "I wonder if she has a feather boa? In any case, she ought to be able to fit into any group. After all, she *is* an actress."

I told her about Glenda's call and impending visit, apologizing for not interrupting her tea event to do so earlier. Her eyebrows rose momentarily.

"Don't worry, it wasn't a collect call. Just one of Glenda's extravagances using Stuart's office telephone." Then I remembered that it was Miss Manley who had partially funded the expenses of Stuart's relatively new office partnership.

We hung up the damp towels and Miss Manley headed for the garden to attack the weeds. I changed into some comfortable clothes and joined her outside a few minutes later.

"Speaking of Highfields, I think I'll take a little walk through the woods up in that direction. It does have a lovely view."

As Miss Manley bent to poke around the flower beds, I passed onto the path behind the house that ended at the Lewises' back garden in one direction and curved away toward town in the other. It was a busy pathway during the day if people chose to use the back way to do an errand rather than take Main Street from their front doors. I passed behind Glenda's house, now occupied by the erstwhile playwright, and could not help looking into his back garden where he sat on a chair facing away from me with a lithe blonde woman on his lap. I was more embarrassed than shocked and turned my head away quickly, fearing either one of them would think I was spying on them. Luckily, they were too busy canoodling to pay attention to whoever walked the path. They were likely unaware that not too long ago, this seemingly sleepy town had roiled from the effects of an affair, a theft and a murder, and gossip could run rampant. It seemed impossible now as I walked down in the direction of town and then veered up onto the quiet path through the woods that led up to Highfields.

"Wait up!" John called, jogging to catch up with me.

"What a surprise," I said.

"Let me walk with you. I desperately need to get out and get some fresh air. The telephone keeps ringing every hour with reports from Bernard about Mr. Ridley's progression to good health."

"He did look awful today, but it seems his assistant fusses excessively."

John laughed at that. "If you had an employer as wealthy as Cash Ridley, it would be in your best interests to make sure he stayed healthy. Forever."

"I suppose," I admitted. I dutifully filled him in on all the information I had gleaned from the late-afternoon gossip session and told him Stuart and Glenda were coming up for the weekend.

"What do you make of his writing?" he asked.

"I'm making a valiant effort to slog through it but I'm afraid it's not my cup of tea," I said.

"I should think not. I've read one and it was terrible! Well, it's overstating it if that's the kind of book you like to read."

"What do you prefer?"

"As you might expect, medical journals—got to keep up with new trends, you know. But I like reading nonfiction about exploration, deeds of heroism, not made-up tales about a fictional character who has arcane knowledge, speaks many languages, can solve any problem, fix any broken machine, not to mention drive it or fly it, gets bashed in the head on a routine basis, shot at least once and still manages to stand up and get the bad guys."

I laughed at his summary. "It sounds like an exhausting thing to read, much less write. I'm afraid I'm stuck at the beginning of the book where a lot of shady, unnamed characters are sneaking around with evil intent."

***

The next morning, we arrived at Dr. Mitchell's office and were surprised to see he was already there and opening the door for us. I had not met him previously but saw he moved deliberately, as if not wanting to exert himself. I felt sorry for someone who had built up this practice over many years and was now forced to abandon it. He took John's hand warmly, clearly fond of him, and grasped mine in both of his, saying how pleased he was to know I was a nurse. Then he slowly took us on a tour of the rooms, with lengthy explanations of what the premises looked like when he first acquired it and the progression of expansion and renovation over the years to its current evolution. He took us last to his office, sat behind the desk with us across from him as if we were patients at the end of a consultation. He looked around at the bookcases.

"I'll be taking a few books but leaving quite a bit behind. My wife insists I take this retirement seriously." He looked wistfully at the volumes accumulated over the years and I felt a pang of compassion for him. Here I was, just starting, full of enthusiasm, with many working years ahead of me and he was on the other end of the spectrum, seeing his possibilities diminishing along with his health.

"Are you and your wife planning a vacation before the end of summer?" I asked.

He turned and his eyes lit up. "Funny you should ask. Just yesterday she suggested we drive up to Maine where we haven't been for years." He smiled at the thought. "Yes, I think it's what we'll be doing. Getting away for a bit." He sighed and, looking down at the desk, opened the top drawer for one last look.

"I think I have everything," he murmured.

"If you've forgotten something or need to get anything, please let me know," John said.

I left to look at the exam room again, just to give them a moment together, but they had headed for the door. We shook hands again, locked the front door and went to our respective vehicles.

"Gosh, that was sad," I commented as we got back into the car. "He seems like such a good, decent man."

"Oh, he is. One of the best."

John paused before starting the engine. "I hope you can come with me to work here in the mornings now that the practice has expanded."

I noticed he stated it rather than asked, but I wasn't surprised.

"I'd be happy to," I said.

We drove over to the Mountain Aire Hotel to check up on Mr. Ridley, even though the assistant had reported great improvement only that morning. It was the perfect day to be driving with the windows down: sunny with a slight breeze that ruffled the heavily leafed-out trees. The roadsides were blooming with wildflowers that looked like wild roses, snapdragons and a purple plant that local people called Joe Pie weed.

With a laugh, I took off my nurse's cap before it blew away into the field of cows methodically chewing their cud. The last time I had made this trip was with Stuart at the wheel after he had had a few drinks, driving much too fast in the darkening night, so I was glad to be able to better appreciate my surroundings this time.

"Do you know anything about Mr. Cash Ridley?" I asked.

"Not really, except I gather that he has a lot of it."

"What?"

"Cash." He laughed. "You saw that car and he has what I assume is a full-time assistant."

"As do you, today," I reminded him.

"True, but unlike Mr. Ridley, I am not being driven in a limousine nor am I in the position to take a month's vacation away from my work."

"Not yet. Someday," I smiled at him, imagining that he would deserve it, and I hoped I would be going with him.

The Mountain Aire was much larger than I had remembered because I had last been there in the evening and then we only ventured into the dining room. I had also been influenced by Stuart's pique at not having gone to the Red Lion Inn instead. The main building of the Mountain Aire had a spacious lobby leading to four stories above and a sizeable wing on either side, one containing the dining room and the other presumably for large events. Behind the building, I could see flat clay tennis courts partially cut into the hills beyond.

An attendant came trotting out pointing toward a nearby parking area, but John explained he was here to see a patient and wouldn't be long. A doctor with his medical bag and a nurse in full kit drew the startled attention of those in the lobby, perhaps imagining some dire mishap to one of the fellow guests. I felt conspicuous walking across the long lobby where owners of the dozen pairs of eyes trained on us pretended to be in conversation or reading a newspaper. But John was calm and discretion itself when asking to be announced to Mr. Ridley.

"The personal or business suite?" the mustachioed clerk behind the front desk asked.

"Wherever he happens to be," was the answer.

The clerk smiled a bit stiffly. "I'll see what I can do." He picked up a telephone, dialed and, turning away, murmured into the receiver. Just as quickly he returned to our attention and wrote the number of the suite on a piece of paper.

"The elevator is just over there," he motioned, handing the paper to John.

The elderly attendant nodded his head, asked for the floor and closed the grille. He was trying hard not to look us over but surely was just as curious as the lobby guests about who was ill.

"Summer colds going around," he stated, looking up at the arrow that showed which floor we were approaching.

"Hmm," said John as the elevator creaked to a halt.

"Good day," the attendant nodded and hesitated to see in which direction we would turn.

"Same to you," John tipped his hat.

The grille shut and the elevator descended.

"Gosh, this is all very cloak and dagger," I said.

"Vacation hotel with everyone looking for something exciting, I suppose."

It appeared that Mr. Ridley had rented at least two suites that took up half of the third floor, as there were only two doors from where we stood to the window at the end of the hall on this side.

John and I exchanged glances.

As we approached the room, the door swung open and Bernard Symington beamed at us, presaging a recovered patient within.

"How good of you to come," he said, ushering us into a foyer that opened to a spacious living room outfitted with the usual hotel furniture but also two desks facing each other at the far end. On the sofa sat Mr. Ridley, smiling through the smoke of his cigarette.

I could feel rather than see John tense up at the realization of dealing with a somewhat overweight man who smoked and may have had a health incident just the day before.

Mr. Ridley perceived the change in the doctor as he rose to shake his hand.

"I know I shouldn't smoke, but these holders," he gestured to the ivory tool into which the cigarette had been placed, "filter out the worst of it."

I could see John wasn't buying that excuse although he just smiled back.

"It's good to see you in better health, sir," he said.

"I feel just dandy!" Mr. Ridley exclaimed.

"May I do a brief examination?" John asked.

"Of course," he boomed back, demonstrating how hearty he was.

Bernard hovered and John shot him a look, indicating privacy would be appreciated. This did not get him out of the room, only to the corner and a seat at the desk that did not have a typewriter on it. He busied himself with shuffling papers while John took Mr. Ridley's heart rate and blood pressure and listened to his breathing front and back with a stethoscope. The patient complied although he seemed a bit too cheery, as if hoping his attitude would allay any possible bad news.

"What do you think? Not so bad for a man of so many years," he said.

"You do appear very much better than yesterday, but your blood pressure is still on the high side." John was being careful to keep his voice low.

"The burden of big business will do that to you." He said it proudly as if poor health was a badge of courage.

John folded his stethoscope back into his bag and asked to sit down.

"Excuse me," I said, thinking to retreat to a couch on the other side of the room but instead going to Bernard's desk, effectively blocking his view of the doctor and patient.

"How long have you been here at the hotel?" I asked.

He tried to look around me unobtrusively and I shifted again and smiled innocently.

"We came up just ten days ago. It is such a relief to be out of the heat of the City."

"I remember. Even a short ride into the suburbs can be cooling." He realized that he could not overhear the other conversation in the room and gave up. Standing, he said, "If you've not been here before, I would be happy to show you around."

"I would be delighted," I said, and his demeanor relaxed.

We took the elevator down to the lobby under the wide-eyed glances of the attendant who had delivered a doctor and a nurse to the upstairs not too long ago and now only the nurse returned. I just smiled at him.

"I had a lovely quiet dinner here recently," I said when we reached the lobby.

Bernard laughed. "That was the dining room, which is reserved for the sedate old-timers. Present company excluded, of course. The action seems to be in the ballroom. Modern, lively music from the Harry Williams Band. He's a bit of a tough character, former lightweight boxer."

I looked surprised.

"The career change was not entirely voluntary. He let rage get the best of him a few too many times."

"Isn't that what the sport is all about?"

"No, that's fighting. You don't get to do that in boxing. And be successful, at least."

He gestured to the opposite wing whose doors at that moment were closed but, when opened by him, revealed a glittering scene of round tables, dramatic lighting and band members in shirtsleeves on the elevated stage taking instruments out of cases.

As we approached, one of the men came down the short flight of steps, smiled at us and shook Bernard's hand.

"How are you, old man?"

"This is Harry Williams, of the Harry Williams Band, of course," Bernard said. "Nurse Burnside." He introduced me.

"Aggie," I corrected. "I had no idea there was entertainment here."

"Oh, yes. No alcohol, of course," he winked. "But we do all right anyway." His broad smile showed off the fashionable chevron mustache that was all the rage and, in his case, also partially covered a scar. "You'll have to come to see us. We're here every night but Sunday. And we've got a terrific new singer. I mean, she is amazing! Really sets the place on fire! Just between you, me and the lamppost, I am hoping she'll come back with us at the end of the summer to New York."

"What about Sophia?" Bernard asked, but Harry had already turned to look back at the bandstand where a young woman had just appeared from the wings, looking at sheet music. Sensing eyes upon her, she turned and gave a dazzling smile and almost skipped to where we stood.

"Harry, Bernard. Oh, I hope no one is sick?" she asked glancing up and down at my uniform with her cornflower blue eyes, suddenly looked distressed.

"No, I'm just here with Doctor Taylor," I said, sidestepping her question and holding out my hand to introduce myself. "I had no idea there was entertainment here. I assume you are the singer?"

"I'm Laura Evans, Lulu actually, filling in for my cousin Sophia Evans who has the worst case of laryngitis. Lucky for her I could get up here quickly and fill in."

"I'll say," Harry added. "She just jumped right into the deep end."

It was hard to tell how old Lulu was; she could have been anywhere from sixteen to twenty-five, but as the object of the compliment she squirmed and tried to blush like a small child.

"Where the hell is Sophia, anyway?" Harry asked, suddenly scowling, his voice sharp.

"What does it matter? She decided to stay inside and rest today. She said that even though she tries not to talk, just thinking about saying something makes her throat hurt."

"Doctor Taylor could take a look at her. He's here, but he's got to get back to West Adams for a two o'clock appointment. I know we have an opening later this afternoon if she would care to stop in."

"Great idea," Harry said, running his hand through the short curly hair on his crown. "I can't believe I have to pay for two singers and only have one."

A bellboy, who might have been Fred, approached us.

"Excuse me, Mr. Symington, but Mr. Ridley was asking for you. He's in the lobby."

As the bassist was wrestling his instrument out of its canvas bag, we made our way from the ballroom and met up with John and Mr. Ridley, who insisted that I call him CR, a very uncomfortable thing from my upbringing. I decided I would refer to him as "sir" instead and if I mumbled it in just the right way it could sound like CR.

He was doing his best to seem youthful and healthy, with hearty guffaws where a simple laugh would do, but perhaps that was his personality. If not, it had to be an exhausting show of bravado.

"Let's have a bit of lunch!" he declared, putting one arm around John and with the other gesturing to the dining room across the way, indicating that Bernard and I should precede them. John tried to dissuade the effusive man by recalling the first appointment of the afternoon in West Adams but was assured that the chef could whip up something quickly and get us back in time. And good to his word, CR snapped his fingers at one of the idle waiters near the door and gave very specific commands about the menu choices and beverages without asking for our preferences. Luckily, he either seemed to enjoy light fare or ordered it for the sake of appeasing what might have been the doctor's recommendations.

"How did you come to hear of the Mountain Aire Hotel?" I asked.

"Somehow it was all the talk of the town this past spring. Where everyone was going to spend the summer. Last year it was Santa Fe and the year before it was Asheville, not that I am a slave to trends and I can assure you, there are people in New York City I would rather *not* see all year round."

Bernard smiled just enough to show amusement without seeming too obsequious, which had to be hard with the force of CR's personality and bombastic behavior.

"Pardon my ignorance," John began, "but I never did ask what sort of business you were in. That is usually one of my first questions to patients, not just to get them comfortable but also to assuage my curiosity. We got off to such a…."

"Dramatic start!" CR said.

"That's one way of putting it," John said.

"To answer your question, I formed the company Ridleyco, manufacturing stainless steel sinks, faucets and hardware. Those porcelain sinks we all grew up with crack, chip and stain but not steel. More builders and homeowners are buying them. They last forever." He put his hand next to his mouth to stage whisper to me, "That's our trademark: *They Last Forever.*"

My guess was he was eyeing me, being young and female, as a potential customer. He had a point about ceramic sinks, however, since I had scrubbed ours back to white with scouring powder many times at home.

"Now here's the interesting part. We've moved into making parts for automobiles. Big contract with Ford Company." He beamed at us around the table. "I have excellent managers heading up my plants—one in Hartford, another in Pittsburgh—although the headquarters is in New York City. It's why I can take a long vacation and bring Bernard and Catherine with me."

"You haven't met her yet," Bernard said. "She's playing tennis. Do you play?"

"I used to," I said. "When I first came up here to work for Doctor Taylor, I thought it would only be for a month and I didn't bring much luggage with me. Then, well, things changed, and I've stayed on." I felt my cheeks begin to blush and looked around as if to see if our lunch was arriving. Luckily, just at that moment, two waiters were hurrying our way with large trays with plates of cottage cheese, salad and fruit.

"See, Doctor, I'm having a healthy diet."

John laughed. "I have a feeling you ordered this only because you knew I would be coming today. Otherwise, what is it usually, steak?"

That brought an acknowledging laugh from CR and Bernard.

"Dig in!"

It was an unusual choice but a light and refreshing change from the staid fare at Miss Manley's. The conversation returned to Ridleyco, its products, its expansion despite the market crash and his pending contracts with several foreign companies. I didn't wonder that he may have suffered from the pressures of work since his depiction of the company was one of constant change and monitoring coupled with his personality, which appeared to necessitate singular control. If things were as he said, the coming years were going to be more stressful although highly successful. But what was the point of the money and prestige if one's health is compromised?

***

We made it back to West Adams with time to spare for the two o'clock appointment, allowing me to sort the mail and attack the billing, although I was uncertain how to handle the medical visit with Mr. Ridley since he had provided us lunch. As I stood to go into John's office and inquire, the reception door opened to Bernard and a stunning woman with auburn hair dressed in a black and white skirt suit. Was this Catherine?

She looked at me and Bernard introduced her.

"I'd like you to meet Sophia Evans. Harry asked me to bring her here as they are rehearsing just now."

She extended her hand to me and nodded.

"Ah, I said. "I think Harry told us you had laryngitis."

She nodded again, smiling, and pulled a small notebook and pencil from her purse when Bernard put his hand on her arm.

"Don't bother writing. I think we all know what the problem is."

She smiled ruefully and John came out of his office to see who had come in.

"Bernard! We meet again. And this must be...."

"Sophia Evans. Nurse Burnside met her cousin, Lulu, earlier today."

"Come into the exam room and we'll see what we can do. Nurse, please get a flashlight."

The exam room door closed while Bernard busied himself looking at a magazine on the table between the chairs in the reception area and I went in search of a flashlight. When I returned to the exam room, John was questioning her in a way that required her only to nod her head for yes or shake it for no. It produced the information that her affliction had come on about a week earlier, seven fingers held up for the days, that she was not prone to laryngitis, that she had been gargling with dissolved aspirin to ease the pain, that she didn't have a cold or cough of any sort. He did the usual exam looking at her tonsils, which I noticed were not inflamed, and then went to the cabinet that held instruments and pulled out one that looked like a dentist's mirror, except that this had a flexible end and a longer handle.

"I'm going to see as far down your throat as I can, and I'll try to gentle, but be aware the mirror may cause a gag reflex. Nurse, would you aim the flashlight, please? Miss Evans, when I ask, I'd like you to vocalize—not sing—but just say ah and then oh, all right?"

She nodded her head and he proceeded carefully, placing the instrument along the soft palate and facing the mirror down her throat. When he asked her to speak, I could just see the vocal cords come together like two curtains closing and opening.

"Does that hurt?" he asked.

She responded, "Mmm," rather than nod her head.

He took the instrument out of her mouth, and I shut the flashlight off.

"Your vocal cords are very inflamed. That's not unusual for someone who uses their voice a lot, as I am sure you do. Does the band provide you with a microphone of any kind?"

She shook her head.

"It could be that you have strained your voice. The immediate solution, of course, is to not speak or sing until the swelling goes down. You don't have a fever, so I don't think it's an infection. But you really must take care of your instrument. Some people who overuse their voice can develop blister-like protrusions that can become calloused and affect the sound quality."

Her eyes grew wide and started to fill with tears. If this was her only livelihood, no wonder she was upset.

"I certainly didn't mean to cause alarm. You're not there yet, by any means, but there are things you can do to lessen the probability of further damage.'

Sophia blinked back her tears and bit her lip.

"Do you smoke?"

She shook her head vehemently.

"Drink alcohol?"

She waggled her hand back and forth in admission.

"Do you have indigestion?"

Sophia looked at him with puzzlement.

John laughed. "I know it seems strange, but sometimes people who have frequent indigestion also have irritation in their throats or vocal cords."

"I didn't know that," I added. Although I shouldn't have spoken, she nodded her head in surprised agreement with my comment.

"I can prescribe you something to ease the soreness; there's a pharmacy in town here, but if it doesn't improve in the next day or two, you might consider seeing a specialist. Let me look at my directory and I'll get the information to you when I go back to the Mountain Aire tomorrow. It will give me a chance to see how you are progressing."

Sophia looked relieved, and she mouthed, "Thank you."

Bernard escorted her back to the big black automobile we had seen just yesterday, and she gave a rather sad wave goodbye.

"I wish I could do something more for her," John said. He went into his office and pulled the New England Medical Directory from a shelf and began his research.

Chapter 4

When I came back from work at four-thirty, Miss Manley was standing in the kitchen, hat on head, handbag at the ready, pulling on her gloves. True to her word, she had telephoned Christa Champion sometime during the day and she was only waiting for me to return to drive her up to Highfields.

"Why don't you go ahead and change, dear? I've noticed that people are sometimes intimidated when they see you in uniform."

"That's my secret weapon," I said, laughing at her astute observation. "I'll be down in a second."

I was glad to take off the cap that required many bobby pins to keep it from slipping on my hopelessly straight hair. Waves and curls were all the fashion among young women, but neither pin curls at night nor curling irons during the day seemed to make much of a difference for me. And I stopped short at a permanent wave, having seen some disastrous results on fellow students in nursing school who had chemically burned their hair, much to the derision of Head Nurse Watson, who shunned any form of vanity.

A floral summer dress looked good with my perforated nurse's shoes, although I had to change my hose before grabbing a cardigan, small hat and handbag and descending to my waiting landlady. We could have just as easily walked up to Highfields but instead succumbed to the luxury of taking Glenda's car to make a bit of an entrance. Backing carefully out of her garage, I could see a curtain in the dining room of Douglas's home twitch with the outline of a woman's face. Was it the same woman I saw before? Or another? We drove slowly along the length of Main Street, Miss Manley waving to her neighbors and friends, and then turned right at the fork and ascended the curving paved road to the big house on the hill.

Situated overlooking the valley and the mountains beyond, Highfields had one of the best vistas in the county. I had been inside during the tenure of the Nashes and admired the stateliness of the two-story brick structure and wondered at the cost of the upkeep. Not only were there many acres of meadow and woodland, but carefully tended lawn and gardens as well, perhaps a score of rooms to be kept dusted and cleaned, housing and food for the staff who accomplished all that work and their salaries as well. Even at the low wages of people in the countryside and during this sad period in our country's economy, the cost of maintaining Highfields must have been staggering. John sometimes teased me about my preoccupation with other peoples' financial situations, but it was due to my early years when my father was suffering the effects of gas during the Great War and had to limit his working hours. He had recovered long ago, but I had acquired the 'wolf at the door' mentality of my mother, mildly anxious that financial fortunes could change at a moment's notice and had thus become aware and curious about the monetary standards of others.

While Mrs. Nash always had a butler or maid answer the door; Christa Champion came to the massive front door herself, whether due to lack of staff or a wish to greet her visitor in person.

"Miss Manley! How good to see you!" She embraced her mother's old friend and introduced herself to me before we, the guests, had a chance to speak.

"Come in! Come in!" Her light brown eyes crinkled as she smiled broadly, an engaging smile not at all artificial. She was far from the feather boa-wearing actress that I had teased Miss Manley about down to the genuine honey-colored hair streaked with grey at the temples and pulled back in a no-nonsense loose bun. The only thing unusual was that she was wearing pants, an uncommon sight in the country where women still wore dresses or skirts even when doing farm labor, except these could hardly be designated as work slacks. They were high-waisted, pleated, full-legged trousers with deep pockets into which she had thrust her hands as she walked us through to the large sitting room with its view of the mountains beyond.

"How lucky that you were able to get Highfields," Miss Manley said. "Of all the grand summer homes in the area, this one has to be the finest."

34

"I couldn't agree more. Come, sit next to me," Christa said, patting the place on the sofa beside where she had been sitting, evidenced by a half-full glass of which we became aware.

"Oops," Christa said. "I am a little embarrassed to say that I've brought my city habits into the country, and it *is* cocktail time. Can I interest you ladies in some refreshment?"

The glance Miss Manley gave me seemed to convey a range of emotions: would she seem too stuffy if she refused? Would Christa think her too worldly if she accepted? To break the ice, I said, "I would say Miss Manley rarely partakes in alcohol, but on this occasion, how could we refuse?"

That seemed to save face all around and Christa got up to ring the servants' bell next to the fireplace. Within moments, Alice, who had evidently been kept on with the new tenants, appeared, her cheery smile showing she recognized us. Although it was probably impertinent to address the servants, I did so, nonetheless.

"How nice to see you still here, Alice."

"Hello, Miss Burnside, Miss Manley. Yes, ma'am?" she inquired of Christa, got instructions and quickly left the room to get the required items.

"Now, tell me, Miss Manley, you and my mother went to school together, is that it?"

As she removed her gloves Miss Manley smiled and tilted her head. "Not exactly. We were of the same age attending different schools when the opportunity came up to have a group tour of Europe with about eight of us girls. Your mother and I hit it off right away, the first day on the boat, and we were roommates for the rest of the trip."

"How delightful! My mother was always admonishing me for being either too dramatic or too daring, so I must know something: was she like that at all? A cut-up? A girl who took chances?"

"Oh, dear, no. We were so well-schooled in behaving ourselves back then, the thought never occurred to us to do anything more daring than ogling the painted women on the streets of Paris. We had been warned that any one of us could be sent home if we did anything improper and, of course, it didn't occur to us how impossible that punishment would be."

"What do you mean?" I asked.

"Well, they couldn't just send one of us home alone, could they? It would mean one of the chaperones would have to accompany us and lose out on the rest of the trip. And the return passage had already been booked—just think of the trouble of re-booking, canceling hotel reservations, and so on. But that was a different time and we young girls paid attention to the admonishments of our elders." She nodded her head to emphasize how the world had changed.

Alice came into the room with a tray of glasses, a bowl of ice and bootleg gin for our cocktail hour. Miss Manley was always more mischievous than anyone might think, and she winked at me in acknowledgment of the little speech she had made and the rule-breaking she was about to indulge in.

"How lucky that you were able to get out of the heat and humidity of New York," I said to Christa, remembering all too well being in the stifling nurses' dorm rooms with only a tiny electric fan that made sleeping barely tolerable.

"I would rather be hot and bothered in the City just now rehearsing a new production, but a major investor backed out this spring and we don't have anything in rehearsal just yet."

"That's dreadful. I didn't realize that productions were so dependent upon investors," I said, once again revealing my interest in all things financial.

Christa had got up to mix the martinis at a small table by the window but said over her shoulder, "My dear, it's *always* about the money. How much do you have to pay to get this particular actor or actress balanced against the ticket sales if you do or don't get them? Should you cut this scene to save money or is it the rollicking end to the second act and can't be eliminated? How many chorus members or dancers in the troupe—but to be honest, that's not the most expensive part of a production. It's advertising! The ads in the newspapers, the posters in the subway stations, pictures on the kiosks. Oh, the expenses are enormous. The more seasoned investors are aware of all these costs but now and again, too often, some naïve person wants to invest in a play or musical for the cachet of it. That is the kiss of death. They expect to attend the rehearsals and have their comments taken seriously, get free tickets for themselves and all their friends, they expect the royal treatment when they appear, are horrified by any expense such as why we pay for a stage manager, and on top of that think the show will run for years and make them a tidy bundle! If it were only so easy!"

"What's so easy?" asked a sonorous voice at the doorway.

"Monty, I was just boring these lovely ladies with the hazards and difficulties of our life on Broadway." She handed the drinks to us and flopped herself on the sofa in a very melodramatic fashion.

"Hello," said the hearty voice of her husband as he extended his hand in greeting. "Monty," he introduced himself.

"My dear husband," Christa said, keeping the aggrieved tone in her voice that she had during her diatribe about the hazards of show business.

He seemed not to notice and went to the bar cart and poured himself a hearty glass of alcohol, then returned to stand in front of the easy chair nearest to me.

"Long life," he said raising his glass. Down went half the drink in one long gulp. I shouldn't have been surprised—as sophisticated New Yorkers, they were likely daily cocktail consumers and with his height and girth, he could probably metabolize half the bottle without blinking an eye while the birdlike Miss Manley was content to take small sips.

Unlike Christa Champion, whose demeanor seemed natural except for her behavior on her husband's entrance, everything about Montgomery Davis shouted, "Theater!" It is not a cliché to describe his reddish-brown hair like a mane: thick and full as a male lion's, matched in color by an extraordinary mustache that required incessant smoothing and pushing out of the way as he spoke. He wore a tweed jacket, surely too warm even in the mild weather of the late afternoon, topped by a paisley ascot at his neck. I had seen Stuart Manley dressed in much the same fashion and I wondered if this had become the style of the creative class in Manhattan because, before that summer, I had never in my life seen anyone wear an ascot except in a movie.

"Dear me, it looks like someone is out of sorts," Monty said to his wife, who had not made eye contact with him since he came into the room.

"Of course, I am out of sorts. We're just kicking around here with no prospects for the fall or the winter theater season. That dreadful—I won't say his name! To hang us out to dry like that."

Addressing Miss Manley and me with a smile, Monty said, "She's just angry because it was probably the last ingenue role she would be able to play." He laughed loudly and swallowed the rest of his drink. "Another?" he asked around the room.

Christa glared at him petulantly, but it didn't seem very genuinely felt. "Of course, that's one reason I am annoyed. It was a fun role, and I could have done it in my sleep." She held out her hand with the empty glass toward him. "Fill up, please."

"But nobody wants to see a performance from a sleepwalker," he said, complying with her request by taking her glass.

"We've only been here a week and haven't figured out what to do with ourselves."

"Speak for yourself," he said jovially. "Someone spilled the beans about us being up here because I have had at least two scripts dropped off by erstwhile auteurs whom I've never heard of before. I certainly don't have time to read them. The tom-toms must have been busy because I've also had a few young women ring the doorbell, if you can believe it, and want to chat about how to get into acting! So many interruptions while I've been on the phone trying to drum up interest with some folks for the next production. But with the heat in the City, it seems everybody is out of town."

"Or avoiding your calls," Christa said.

"Where do most of your friends go to cool off?" Miss Manley asked.

"Some go to the Poconos, others farther north to the Adirondacks, still others go out to Long Island to the beach towns."

"All of that sounds lovely," I said. "But it's nice here, too. Cool evenings, beautiful scenery, and there's even a bit of nightlife at the Mountain Aire Hotel."

"Actually, we've been. It was lucky that I packed evening clothes," Christa said.

"This from a woman who originally wanted to have a do-nothing vacation," he said anticipating her reaction and response.

"Really, Monty! You can't keep me working my fingers to the bone half the year and on the shelf the other six months."

"I fail to see how acting involves your fingers," he said, handing her a new drink. "Actually, that young singer is bursting with talent. I want to see her again and talk to her before someone else snatches her up."

"I think that has already happened. She seems ensconced in the Harry Williams Band."

"I know, but that's just a summer engagement," Monty said.

"I heard Harry say he wanted to make sure she stayed with them to the end of the season," I said, wanting to show I was in the know with local gossip.

"I can offer her a much better opportunity. Broadway! I can make her a star!"

"Monty, you are getting ahead of yourself as usual. We don't even have a property to produce. And I might not be fifteen or however old that girl is, but there's life in me yet!" Christa said with emphasis.

"Of course, dear, I certainly didn't mean that you should be put out to pasture."

Christa looked over at Miss Manley and me. "That's a dreadful expression. You make me sound like an old horse." She pouted.

"I'm sorry, love," he said, coming behind to kiss her on the top of the head. "But sometimes you can be a nag."

She slapped the hand on her shoulder playfully.

"When we were there for dinner not so long ago, I didn't realize there was a ballroom that serves as a kind of nightclub in the evenings," Miss Manley said.

Christa clapped her hands. "Let's *all* go!"

"What, now?" Monty asked.

"I meant let's make an evening of it soon."

"I think a nightclub is more of a young person's adventure," Miss Manley said.

All three of us objected to her implication of being elderly, but she persisted. "My nephew and his wife are coming for the weekend. Perhaps they'd like to join you."

After another round of chit chat, Miss Manley and I left, one drink apiece being enough for our timid ability to indulge. We laughed most of the way home—and not because of the martinis—but due to what must be the nature of their marital discourse with one complaining and the other fueling the fire by teasing. It was almost like watching a play, but perhaps the only way they could communicate was by playing their characters. I made sure that the two of us each had a peppermint before entering the back door in case Annie was still there; luckily, she had her hat on and was just walking out the front door.

"Dinner's in the oven, ready to come out in ten minutes. I'm sorry, I've got to dash," she said, rushing out the door.

"In that case, I'll just pop next door and ask Nina a question," I said, leaving Miss Manley to remove her hat and gloves before opening the oven door and peering inside.

The Lewises lived next door and like other residents of West Adams, I had got into the habit of dropping in unannounced; however, unlike a true native, I always knocked on the door first, something Elsie found strange and, by her grumpy face, an annoying interruption in her work.

"Hello, is Mrs. Lewis in?"

She jerked her head over her shoulder indicating the sitting room and that's where I found Nina reading the evening paper with her teenage nephew Roger scanning the sports pages.

"Hello, Aggie," she said, with Roger mumbling, "Hullo."

"Is everyone out of sorts here tonight?" I said in a whisper, looking toward the kitchen, not wanting to get on Elsie's bad side, which was known to be ferocious.

"Elsie is put out because Roger told her he would not be eating dinner with us tonight, when in fact he is, and now she thinks there won't be enough. And Roger is annoyed because we won't let him go to the Mountain Aire Hotel *again*." She made a funny expression that I couldn't interpret.

"What's at the Mountain Aire?" I remembered his recent fascination with tennis and asked if it was that. She gave me a barely disguised, withering look.

"Nothing quite so tame, I'm afraid. It's that girl."

"Oh, really," Roger said, folding the paper noisily, throwing it down on the hassock and stomping out of the room.

Nina waited until his footsteps disappeared up the stairs. "He's got a mad crush on the singer at the hotel," she said.

There was no doubt Sophia Evans was a beautiful woman, but I thought certainly out of Roger's league as a seventeen-year-old. But perhaps that was the attraction.

"Sophia? Really?" I asked.

"No, no. Lulu Evans, although her stage name is Laura Evans. Really, what teenager has a stage name? He is completely gaga over her, as is his friend Bobby Haynes." She sighed and folded the paper back to its original shape.

"Is Bobby the one with the car?"

"Yes, yes. It's always about someone with a car. Not only that but now Roger says he got a job there until school starts in the fall!"

Reverend Lewis came in from his study at that point, roused from reading or writing in his study by the commotion on the stairs.

"A job!" He stopped short, not having heard me come in earlier. "How nice to see you, Aggie." He looked at his wife and repeated, "A job! Roger? That's wonderful."

Nina's mouth fell open. "I agree a job would be a wonderful thing but not *there*."

He laughed long and hard and Nina's face grew pink with indignation.

"I'm the one who should be offended about him working in a nightclub, not you." He went over and kissed her on the forehead

"Nightclub! He said he would be grooming the tennis courts among other odd jobs. Who said anything about a nightclub?" she asked.

"Is that why you're upset?" Reverend Lewis asked.

"It's not actually a nightclub, per se," I said. "Of course, no alcohol is served."

Nina's head turned from her husband to me and back again. "The only reason he is interested in a job there is so that he can ogle that girl."

I stood up. "I'll leave you two to chat."

"I'm sorry, I interrupted," the reverend said, motioning me to sit down again, only too glad to be rescued from the family conversation.

"Not at all, but Nina, I was wondering if you could recommend a dress shop in Pittsfield. I only brought one fancy dress with me from home and…."

"And you're going to the Mountain Aire, aren't you?" she asked sounding wounded.

"Yes, I think the doctor and I will be going sometime this weekend."

"Aggie, I'll write down some suggestions if you want to pick up the list tomorrow." Somehow, the mention of the doctor's name mollified her suspicions about the place, and she turned to her husband and said as if to close the discussion, "Well, I expect we'll just have to go sometime ourselves."

Chapter 5

CR had invited us to dinner for the next night and I took the afternoon off to drive the winding road to Pittsfield to shop for what I hoped was a glamorous dress. The bus was reliable transportation but slow as it halted to let people off near their homes rather than at any central stop, so I opted to drive Glenda's car instead and being behind the wheel on a different roadway was a new and unnerving experience. Poking along Main Street was one thing but quite another having to maintain a good pace while going around the curves and wondering if I was going too fast or too slowly. It was a relief to reach the outskirts of the city, park the car and look for the first dress shop on the list. The store was not large but the selection bounteous compared to the Misses Smith establishment in West Adams and the saleswoman had a good eye for what would suit my figure and complexion so that less than an hour later I was on my way home.

I don't know why I was nervous about the evening ahead; I had been in CR and Bernard's company before, but both times I had my nurse identity, which was professional and competent. Now I might be expected to have my young woman's identity on display, and I wasn't confident as to what that should be. Certainly, the dress was designed to show off my shape to advantage without being revealing and I hoped it would create the impression of someone with taste and discretion. I had a thin gold necklace and matching bracelet to wear and restrained makeup on, but the hair— oh, the hair. It would just have to be Aggie hair, straight as could be, perhaps pulled back on one side with a clip. That did the trick, and I thought it added a note of elegance.

A few minutes before John came over, Nina popped in to see my outfit and she was impressed.

"The color is perfect. And the fit! It looks as if you didn't need any alterations."

"I was lucky to find something with the right length for my height."

Nina shook her head at me. "Aggie, you make it sound that being tall is a deficit, but you are statuesque."

"Goodness, you make it sound like playing Statues." I struck a frozen pose as Miss Manley came into the sitting room.

"Are you quite all right?" she asked me.

"Just practicing being statuesque."

***

John thoughtfully drove with the windows rolled up so as not to destroy my hairstyle, if you could call it that. He looked over at me several times in surprise and admiration and took my hand at one point before having to release it to downshift around a corner. It was a much more pleasant ride than the one with Stuart Manley, where we were rolling from side to side as he took the corners so quickly. John and I had had several dates, going to the movies in Adams, a few tame hikes on the weekend and a home-cooked dinner at his house—a surprise from a bachelor! We had never had such a formal outing and it was exciting to know that our being together in a public space would speak volumes about our developing relationship. In some ways that was exhilarating, but I wondered if the locals would think it happened too quickly or that I was fast woman.

As it turned out, very few locals were in the dining room at the Mountain Aire that evening as far as I could tell. CR had insisted that we join him and his party for dinner, his treat naturally, and I had earlier brought up to John the curious dilemma of billing his patient after he was paying for our meals. John reassured me that it was unusual but that our host not only had money to burn and loved to spend it on others, but that someone in the bank in Adams told him Cash Ridley had made an offer to buy the hotel from the Fosters. How funny that starting my work in what I thought was a poky practice serving the farmers and townspeople in a little town in the Berkshires had changed so quickly into an almost-full-time job and hobnobbing with Broadway people and giants in industry.

We met CR in the lobby accompanied by Bernard, as usual, and Catherine Hastings, the secretary, a well-tanned young woman with a strong handshake. I asked her about tennis lessons, and she praised the hotel's professional coach effusively, saying her game had improved with his assistance.

"It helps that I just have to get up a little early and the courts are right here rather than in Manhattan where one has to belong to a club—which I do—and then reserve a court days in advance, not knowing what my work demands will be."

"And Heaven knows, I am such a demanding boss!" CR said with a laugh as we were shown to the best table facing broad windows with a view of the mountains.

Catherine colored slightly and nervously touched the small cross she wore on a chain around her neck. "Oh, CR, you know I didn't mean you!"

He patted her on the shoulder and chortled, then was seated at the head of the table by the maître d' so his position had the best view, Catherine to one side, I to the other with John and Bernard at the other end. It was curious that this man who had an outsized ego chose to sit with his back to the room; it showed me that he was self-confident to a degree that he didn't need others in the room to notice him, where he sat, or with whom.

I opened my menu to find that there were no prices next to any of the selections. Was this some kind of error? Our menus were not like this the last time I was here because I remember Stuart's financial situation and, although he was treating his aunt, Glenda and me to dinner, I didn't want to order the most expensive thing. This time, I looked over to John and saw he was briefly puzzled as well, but Bernard and Catherine were engrossed in the many choices, clearly used to CR's habits and largesse. I saw the Maine lobster and was tempted but knew it was a lot to eat, impossible to manage without making a mess, and I was not going to suffer having a bib put around my neck as they did in restaurants on the coast. I glanced around and didn't see anyone else having lobster so put the idea firmly aside.

"What do you recommend?" John asked.

"Bernard and Catherine have their preferences, eating all their meals here, but if this is the first time you've been here, I would strongly suggest the filet mignon."

"Thank you," said John and closed his menu.

"I'll have the same," I said. I knew what it was but had never had it at home, my mother's being a frugal housewife despite our solid financial circumstances.

The waiter and the maître d' reappeared and asked CR many questions while I looked at all the other offerings: soup, appetizers, salads and desserts. Then they turned their attention to me, and I couldn't think of anything else to order but tomato juice to start and then the filet mignon, as suggested by CR.

"So that's how you keep your trim figure!" CR said.

"I do run her off her feet quite a bit at the practice," John joked.

Around the table, the orders were given and before anyone mentioned beverages, another waiter brought out from his waistcoat a medium-sized bottle of a clear liquid that he poured into the short glasses set before us. Catherine put her hand over her glass and John shook his head to refuse.

"Oh, come on, Doctor. Catherine may have religious reasons to refuse, but you?"

"I'm driving tonight," he said in response, although I knew he regretted not having some of what must be a high-quality alcohol.

The three of us who partook raised our glasses and, if it was superior liquor, I couldn't say but it was very strong, and I apologized before asking to have some water added to it.

That made CR laugh, and as I thought about it, almost everything was amusing to him.

"Atta girl!"

The men had ordered appetizers and when they were brought out, a stout man in evening dress came to table and shook CR's hand and asked how the meal was progressing. He was introduced to us as George Foster, Senior, the owner of the hotel. If it were true that CR wanted to acquire the place, it made perfect business sense that Mr. Foster would make sure the meal was to everyone's pleasure.

"I had heard so much about this place from friends in the City," CR said. "But I never imagined it would exceed my expectations."

"Thank you, CR," Mr. Foster responded. "But the credit really goes to Junior, who has spent the best part of a year working to enhance our little part of the world. He's the one who discovered the Harry Williams Band in New York after all." He glanced around the table, subtly taking note of who was eating what, and then smiled. "I'll leave you to enjoy your meal."

It was a pleasant dinner with interesting conversations about the history of the area and the many connections that CR had made in the past relating to this section of Massachusetts. We were there quite some time because after the main course a cart was brought out with a variety of elaborate cakes and pastries from which to choose. Then coffee. Just as the coffee was being poured, a voice came from behind our host.

"CR! What a charming party!" It was the singer from Harry Williams' band.

"Laura! Come join us."

"Oh, I can't."

"What—you're suitably dressed."

"This old thing?" She laughed. "Can't. I have to change. Going on pretty soon."

"I'd like to introduce…," CR began.

"I've met Nurse Burnside, but not Doctor Taylor. Sophia told me all about you. I see what she meant." She winked at him, and I was amused to see he could be so uncomfortable as to blush.

She wrinkled her nose and giggled in what I imagine she thought was a cute fashion and CR thought the entire interaction was hilarious. Bernard and Catherine nodded acknowledgment of her presence and looked down at what remained on the plates in front of them.

"You are coming to the show?" she asked.

"Naturally, dear," CR said, putting his arm around her waist. Now, everyone at the table was uncomfortable, not just his employees, who had looked up, eyebrows raised, then looked away.

"Ta-ta," she said, giving a wave and walking off.

The men's conversation started up again and, when I excused myself to the powder room, Catherine rose to show me where it was.

"I do admire how fit you are," I said.

"I love playing tennis and being here allows me to have a daily swim, as well."

"My only exercise lately has been walking to and from work, which is ridiculous because the doctor's office is almost next door."

"I shouldn't worry if I were you. It seems you have a naturally slim figure that you'll keep all your life."

I certainly hoped she was right.

"Why don't you join me for a set sometime soon?"

"What a wonderful idea," I said. "I suppose there will be an extra racket for me somehow."

We returned to the dining room minutes later, arm in arm, and the men got up to escort us across the lobby to the ballroom.

"We'd better hurry or we won't get the best table," CR said, chuckling.

We all smiled knowing that Bernard had likely booked the best table, and we were correct: front and center of the dance floor with the bandstand behind which the musicians adjusted their chairs, the clarinet player fidgeted with his reed, the bassist stood at attention next to his instrument, the drummer poised and Harry Williams smiled broadly at the entrance of our group. Once we were seated, Harry nodded, and the evening's music began.

The band started out playing a lively version of *When You're Smiling,* and several couples immediately got up and fox-trotted across the smooth floor. CR was enjoying himself, tapping his fingers in time to the music and clapping enthusiastically when the number was over. More couples joined the original group as the performers swung into a rendition of *Carolina Moon*. Bernard asked me to dance, and we were swept into the romantic rhythm as he held me more closely than I would have liked, presumably so we could keep up a conversation.

"How did you come to work for Mr. Ridley?" I asked.

"This may come as a surprise, but I was married to his daughter, Constance."

That didn't explain if the working situation existed before or after his marriage, and I was speechless wondering where she was and why no one had mentioned her existence before.

"Unlike her name, she was not very constant and ran off with another man. Don't look at me with pity, dear Aggie. CR was so furious that he demanded we divorce, and she was summarily cut out of his will. He and I never speak about her."

"I'm sorry I asked." And truly, I was.

"And what about you? How did you come to work in this part of the world?" He trained his eyes on me and I noticed they were neither brown, nor grey, nor green, but some mixture of the three, changing color somewhat as we danced in and out of the light in the room.

I told him my brief story, the expansion of John's practice and the resultant permanency of my position. For something to say, I expanded on my living situation, Miss Manley and the elderly women of the town.

"They sound ferocious!"

"Not at all, I don't intend to make them sound mean-spirited. They just like to gossip, and other people are the topic, that's all. Now that there is a famous couple up at Highfields, it adds spice to their conversations."

Bernard asked who the couple was and when I told him, he put his head back and laughed. "Monty and Christa! CR will love to hear that as he knows them well."

The music stopped, we returned to the table while Harry came to what must be a newly purchased microphone to announce a brief break and then the band would return with Laura Evans. There were murmurs of excitement and I, too, was caught up in the moment of anticipation. One of the waiters brought an additional chair to our table and Sophia Evans appeared, nodded her head to us all while pointing at her throat to indicate she was still not talking and sat down. CR patted her on the shoulder and, as people do when others can't talk, pantomimed pouring her a drink. She looked over at John as if asking permission and he nodded as if to say, "It won't hurt."

Drinks were poured all around, with Catherine and John abstaining, and we began to talk about how impressed we were with the band.

"Wait until you hear Laura," CR said.

It was an unintentionally cruel thing to say considering the only reason Laura had a chance to be performing here was the ill luck of her cousin's loss of voice.

John leaned close to me and whispered, "It looks like someone else can't wait to hear Laura," indicating with a glance Roger, his friend Bobby and a bellboy we had seen earlier standing just outside the ballroom doors.

"Did you manage to get an appointment with that specialist?" I asked Sophia.

She nodded her head, smiled at John and mouthed, *"Thank you."*

"I haven't met him, but I understand he's very good," John said.

"What's that?" CR asked and Bernard explained the outcome of her doctor's visit and the hope that she could get some resolution to her problem.

We chatted for the remainder of the band's short performance break, and they returned to applause, with Lulu following them out in a sparkling, low-cut, tight-fitting dress that flared out below the knees, artfully applied makeup and a gardenia behind one ear. The applause continued, CR clapping heavily. I could see Sophia was less enthusiastic in her response, seeing her replacement getting such an effusive reception.

"Thank you," Lulu said, looking down humbly, before sweetly singing the introduction to *I Can't Give You Anything but Love,* then stopping at the last note and looking down demurely. In a complete change of pace, Harry struck several chords at a rapid pace, Lulu snapped her head up and delivered a fast and rousing rendition of the song with slight hip and shoulder shaking as she belted out the song. I was taken aback by the sheer impact of her performance and surprised that it struck me so viscerally, but looking at the others around the table, except Sophia, they seemed to have the same reaction. And it was not limited to us alone because when she finished, the ballroom erupted in extended applause.

"That was something," murmured John, his eyebrows almost up to his hairline.

The next song was a ballad, and she had the audience in the palm of her hand as she sang *Exactly Like You*. Again, extended clapping.

"Isn't she terrific?" CR said, practically pounding the table in enthusiasm.

Her set was about twenty minutes long and then she departed to let the band have the stage to themselves so couples could dance, and John and I took advantage of the opportunity.

"I don't think I've ever seen anything like that performance," I said.

"I guessed she might be a firecracker, but wow!" John agreed.

He twirled me around facing our table and I saw Lulu standing next to CR chatting with him while he looked up at her with the face of a lovesick teenager. Lulu bent closer to say something to him before leaving. Her exit was followed closely by most people in the room, some with admiration, some with curiosity, some indifferent and a few with pure hatred.

I had a premonition that this was not going to end well.

Chapter 6

We had such a full schedule the next day with school physicals, a colicky baby and the regular lumbago patient that I didn't have time to take a breath until almost five-thirty.

John and I closed up the office, both of us bone-tired from the constant influx of patients so I made my way home to a bath and dinner.

The evenings were still long this far north, and Miss Manley and I took advantage of the fading light to sit out in the garden and listen to birdsong in the dusk.

"I didn't have a chance to tell you that Christa was a big hit today at tea at Mrs. Rockmore's."

"I certainly hope everyone was polite."

"Of course!" Miss Manley said. "And Christa was charm itself, gushing about gardens, and inquiring what sights she and Monty ought to see, and how enchanting West Adams is."

"That was laying it on a bit thick, don't you think?"

"Perhaps, but the ladies have this strange notion that city folk are naïve in their own way and so accepted the fact that perhaps our quiet little town is impressive because of its simplicity."

"Did anyone ask her to perform one of her famous scenes?" I giggled at the thought.

"I'm sure the thought was on someone's mind; however, everyone was too polite to suggest it. The talk was all about young Mona Strathern threatening to run away to New York."

"Mrs. Strathern told you that?" That surprised me as I was under the impression that, while gossip was shared here, an embarrassing personal situation would be kept to oneself as long as possible. And a runaway daughter ranked high on the list of such events.

"Heavens, no. She wasn't there. I believe she has been staying close to home to keep Mona on a short leash."

We heard the rumble of a car pulling up in front of the Lewises' house and shortly thereafter, Roger and his friend Bobby walked between the two houses to the backyard.

"Hullo, everyone," Roger said, his curly hair blown back from the recent drive.

"I don't think you've met Miss Burnside," he said, introducing to me his friend whom I knew only by reputation as the boy with the car. He had a great shock of red hair and freckles, a firm handshake and a mischievous smile.

"So, you are Roger's partner in crime," I said.

"Guilty as charged!" Both young men thought the joke funny and asked to join us, sitting on the bench next to Miss Manley.

"What did you think of the performance at the Mountain Aire last night?" I asked.

They started talking at the same time, each trying to outdo the other with adjectives in a fantastic crescendo of superlatives that left them breathless and the two of us laughing at their exuberance.

"And how is your new job, Roger?"

"It's swell! You know how I love tennis so it's great to watch the pro teaching the guests. I've picked up some great tips on how to improve my serve. And this afternoon, they were short one for a doubles match and I got to play."

"Talk about tips," Bobby whispered flamboyantly.

"Yes, and the couple actually gave me some money." He seemed incredulous.

The kitchen screen door to Glenda's house slammed loudly and her tenant, Douglas, made his way to Miss Manley's yard.

"What's all the commotion?" he asked, in a jolly tone.

"Just youth," Miss Manley said. "Come join us, Mr. Martin." She motioned to the empty lawn chair.

"Douglas," he corrected, moving hesitantly in our direction.

"Where have you been lately?" Roger asked. "We haven't seen you in ages."

"Roger!" Miss Manley chided his outspoken comment.

"Writing," he answered in a glum tone.

We knew from observation that he was a bit of a night owl in his habits, but his pallor made him look as if he hadn't seen the sun in days. His deep-set eyes in an angular face accentuated the effect of ill health or exhaustion.

"Are you writing the Great American Novel?" Bobby asked.

"Oh, how I wish. That's where the money is. I've written several plays but this one is driving me to distraction."

"What seems to be the problem?" Miss Manley asked, tipping her head to one side.

Douglas ran his fingers through his hair. "Everything. Simply everything."

There didn't seem to be a suitable response or follow-up question to that sad statement that stunned us into silence.

"Say," Roger began, "why don't you...," but he was stopped mid-sentence by Douglas continuing his lament.

"I just don't know whether it's worth it or whether I should just chuck it altogether."

I thought that his chucking it could mean Glenda would lose a tenant, a source of income that she would regret losing.

"I imagine it's a competitive field," I suggested.

"Hah! It's who you know, and it appears that I don't know the right folks. I found out that Montgomery Davis was staying in the house on the hill, so I dropped off one of my works with a charming introductory note. Oh, how I hate having to grovel!"

The body language of the rest of us indicated how uncomfortable it was to be the audience for his self-loathing.

"But you have an established profession. Think of us young men who haven't had a chance to accomplish anything yet and are looked down on by older people because of it," Roger said.

"That's not true," Miss Manley said. "We certainly don't look down on you and you have a lifetime to achieve great things."

"It's true. Just look at Cash Ridley. He snaps his fingers at people who work at Mountain Aire like he owns the place."

I hated to burst his balloon, but I said, "Actually, I understand he is about to own it."

"The Fosters intend to sell it?" Miss Manley asked.

"That's what I heard," I replied.

Bobby piped up. "And all the old goats chasing the young girls around getting their attention, leaving us out in the cold."

Roger huffed in agreement and irritation at the indignity of it all.

"Whatever do you mean?" I asked, stunned at how injured they both sounded.

"Laura Evans," they answered in unison, looking sheepish.

I suddenly felt rather old as I regarded their damaged egos as a ridiculous notion.

"And do you know what?" Douglas said rather than asked. We all turned in his direction at this out-of-sequence remark. "Monty Davis had the audacity to have some servant call so I could pick up my 'package.' Unread!"

"Are you sure he didn't read it?" Miss Manley asked.

"It is not an assumption. He had it for a mere two days and I could tell from the look of the paper that he made it through the first eight pages or so before giving up. Didn't even give me any notes or suggestions, let alone encouragement."

"Boy, that stinks," Bobby said. It seems the young men's trouble attracting a certain singer's attention was not as devastating as the wretched face of the playwright who wouldn't see his masterpiece produced.

Douglas stood suddenly. "That pompous ass. I'm going to drown my sorrows now, if you'll excuse me."

"Can we help?" Roger asked, following the older man back through Glenda's back garden, Bobby trailing at his heels to join them in self-pity. We shook our heads at the audacity of the two younger men who couldn't obtain alcohol any other way.

"At least Douglas has a girlfriend to keep him company and perhaps can put him in a better state of mind," Miss Manley said.

"Girlfriend? I haven't been spying on him, but I think I have seen him with at least two different women in the short time he's been here," I said.

"Oh, dear. I hope neither of them was Mona."

Chapter 7

A crash and an apology from Annie started the morning on Friday as she struggled up the stairs with a full complement of cleaning supplies and dragging a vacuum to ready the guest room for Stuart and Glenda, who were expected that night. Miss Manley insisted on a floor to ceiling dusting, sweeping and vacuuming each time they visited although the room got no use in the meantime and to my knowledge Stuart had been the only guest over the years. Nonetheless, the scrape of wood on wood screeched as Annie moved the bureau and then the bed to sweep underneath. I made sure to be washed, dressed and downstairs before the commotion of the vacuum began.

I remembered my first leisurely month being able to sleep in since I only worked in the afternoons. The leap from part-time to full-time was not as taxing as I had imagined but it left little opportunity to do errands and I knew I was remiss in answering letters from my former classmates as well as family. Perhaps I would catch up this weekend while Miss Manley was occupied with her nephew and Glenda as long as they didn't include me in their plans.

Promptly at eight-thirty, I opened the door to the reception room at the doctor's office and surveyed what I might need to take with me to Adams.

"Good morning, Aggie," John said, poking his head around the door from the kitchen of his residence that led into the business portion of the house.

"Good morning. Are we expecting a busy day?" I asked him.

"You tell me," he said, picking up the appointment book and seeing that there were a few names jotted down. Standing that close to me I detected the sandalwood scent of his shaving soap and it made me smile. "You know Fridays. Whatever ails you can wait until the end of the week. Doc Taylor has got nothing else to do!"

"Actually, Doc Taylor will have to cut short his afternoon in order to get ready for our evening at the Mountain Aire." I searched in the drawer for a notebook.

John groaned. "It's a fun place, but not my idea of a relaxing evening."

"It's not meant to be relaxing. It's entertainment. At least we don't have to sit through a long, drawn-out meal there. Bernard and Catherine aren't the liveliest conversationalists."

"How can they be when CR monopolizes the conversation? Bernard won't be there anyway. He's taking Sofia down to Hartford for an afternoon appointment to see the ear, nose and throat specialist. I expect they'll be back after dark."

John went back to get his jacket and hat while I wondered if Bernard had a thing for Sofia or the other way around. They were both attractive, youngish and in each other's company a lot. Bernard had a secure position with Cash Ridley and, judging by his comments about his former marriage, might stand to inherit from his boss as well. Sofia might have had a glamorous occupation that was now in jeopardy from two fronts: her vocal damage and being upstaged by her cousin. There I was again, speculating about people, their finances and their motivations.

It was a busy Friday at both locations, with several walk-ins at each place but luckily no broken bones or trauma to contend with. We finished up a little after five o'clock, giving us both time to have a light dinner at our respective homes and get ready for the dazzling night ahead. I envied John's easy choice of a dinner jacket while I was puzzling over the dilemma of re-wearing the dress I had just bought or relying on one that hadn't been seen by the residents of the Mountain Aire. Then I had to laugh at myself for imagining that anyone cared what a 'townie,' as Roger said the guests referred to the local folks, was wearing. I decided to go with the dress that Miss Smith had altered for me earlier in the summer since it fit so well. But first, dinner with Miss Manley.

Annie had made us poached fish with a light cream sauce and a sliced tomato salad, perfect for a summer meal. It was too bad that Miss Manley wasn't joining us at the hotel, but she wanted to be at home when Stuart and Glenda arrived, a reasonable excuse, but I expect a nightclub, as everyone kept referring to it, was likely not her first choice. I shouldn't have pre-judged her because I simply could not imagine Miss Manley as a young woman.

"What sort of entertainment did you use to enjoy?" It just sort of popped out of my mouth.

"I imagine you think all we did was square dance or sing hymns?" she asked with a mischievous glint in her eye.

"Did you have dance halls around here?"

That term made her laugh. "I don't really know. Young women who were sent off to boarding school when I was young were not supposed to know about dance halls or roadhouses. Of course, that was before Prohibition, so drinking was not illegal or scandalous. In our set, we had chaperoned evening parties with the boys from nearby schools. It was all tightly supervised, and the dances then were formal waltzes—nothing like the athletic exhibitions that dancing is today."

I looked down to hide my smile at her terminology.

"We also had what was called a tea dance in the late afternoon, again watched like hawks by the teachers lest anyone dance too close."

"Well, some things haven't changed. Our dancing techniques may have been different, but we had teachers and parents watching from the sidelines. And then the quiz on the way home: 'Who was that rather handsome young man you danced with toward the end?' That meant he was suitable although my parents deemed me much too young to go out on a real date until I was sixteen."

Miss Manley smiled at my choice of words. "We didn't go out on dates back then, at least not at school, and not when I came home to West Adams. Someone would come calling, meaning he would be at your house, in your sitting room, chatting with you and your parents."

That sounded safe and very boring. But what else was there to do in this small town but visit other friends, play music or go for a walk. It made me wonder why Miss Manley never married, but that question was for another day.

I glanced at my watch and excused myself to change for the evening ahead. We were taking the reverend and Nina with us, a great treat for her who had heard so much about the hotel and the entertainment. I had the impression that the reverend was less enthusiastic—what would some of the parishioners say, not that many or any would be in attendance—but he had given in to his wife's wishes. I certainly hoped he wasn't going to wear his dog collar. That would put a damper on the evening.

I was coming down the stairs when the front doorbell rang, making me wonder who it could be. Surely not a neighbor, who would just come in the back door or through the French doors in the living room. I opened the door to the reverend and Nina, who thought it only appropriate under the circumstances to come in the front way. She was outfitted in a stunning pink dress, bringing out the roses in her cheeks, and she informed me the man in the dinner jacket accompanying her was to be addressed as Robert, certainly not the reverend.

"Very well," I said skeptically.

"And I won't call you Nurse Burnside."

"All right then," I agreed.

John appeared a few minutes later and I took his arm as we walked out to the car he had pulled into the driveway, and soon we were off on what felt like a sophisticated evening, although it was the only entertainment for miles around. A slight drizzle slowed down our progress through town but let up as we left for the main road toward the hotel.

"I wonder what Mrs. Rockmore will think of the band?" John asked.

I could feel the reverend, I mean, Robert, stiffen in the back seat, then lean forward. "Is she really going to be there?" he asked.

Picking up John's playful mood, I added, "It will be fun to see the tea group cutting a rug."

Nina laughed heartily and pulled her husband back beside her. "Really, you two! Actually, we haven't danced in years," she said.

"It hasn't been years, I'm sure," Robert said.

"It was at the coming-out party for what's-her-name."

He grunted, indicating he couldn't remember who that was either.

We rode in silence for the rest of the trip, coming down into the shallow valley toward the hotel lit up, dramatically illuminating the lawns and gardens.

"It does look lovely," Nina said. "Aggie, you said the food was wonderful, but is the dining room expensive?"

"I don't know. Mr. Ridley paid for our meal both times, so I don't have a clue."

There were two young men, one of them Fred, according to Nina, who was available to park the car. The young man recognized the reverend and his wife, greeted them politely but all the same his eyebrows shot up at the thought of them stepping into the place.

I felt very grown-up holding up my long skirt slightly to walk up the stairway to the lobby, heads turning when we went toward the ballroom, and wondered if any of the lobby sitters recognized me in my different attire. The music drifted out each time the ballroom door was opened, and we were hit with a blast as we went through into the crowded and smoky space.

"My goodness, this is popular!" Nina commented as we were escorted to a table by the side of the bandstand, a good vantage point but certainly not the prime location that Cash Ridley had once again staked out for himself. He saw us come in and waved, then waited until we were seated to approach to greet us.

"I'm so glad you can't keep away!"

John stood to shake hands and introduced Robert and Nina, as they now were, and Cash bent to kiss her hand, which surprised all of us. Realizing that I was also at the table he trotted around, quite a feat considering his size, and took my hand and kissed it as well.

"The lovely Aggie," he said.

"When does Laura perform?" I asked him.

"Fairly soon, I believe. She's got two shows tonight with a break in between. I'll bring her over to say hello. I've got Monty Davis and Christa sitting with me," he continued gesturing back to his table with his hand. Christa turned at that point, I waved to her, and she gave me a generous smile in return.

"I didn't know you were acquainted," Cash said.

"We met this week up at Highfields through my landlady, Miss Manley. Monty and Christa seem an interesting couple."

"Yes, old friends from Manhattan. But we're going to talk business tonight—can't help myself! We'll meet up at the break."

The band struck up another number and the dance floor filled while we chatted and watched the others, thinking to engage in the next number that turned out to be when Lulu came out from the wings in a different dress from her previous performance but one no less sparkly and striking, accented by a gardenia in her hair. Many in the crowd began to applaud and we joined in, Nina looking at me with surprise at the enthusiastic response in the room before a note was sung.

Harry Williams raised his hand, the band began to play and the melody to *Glow Worm* began, a familiar and happy song from childhood that was transformed into a sultry, enticing invitation as Lulu moved in time to the music, shaking her shoulders slightly and making eye contact with individual men in the audience. Nina looked over at me, wide-eyed at the innocent song delivered in that sexy manner, and I gave her a 'What did I tell you?' look in return. The men did not notice our silent communication; their eyes were focused on the singer's stunning delivery.

The last phrase of the song brought her arms up in the air and a playful smile to her lips amid thunderous applause. The reaction was extraordinary, with CR lapping it up since he apparently considered her his protégé while Harry Williams was smiling stiffly, probably not too pleased to realize the possessiveness of the other man. Still, her performance had been electric; the crowd wanted more, and she obliged. Whether the song was a ballad or a jaunty tune, men and women alike were enthralled and clapped wildly after each song. Finally, she got to the last of her set, blew kisses at all of us in the room and walked off to the wings. But, seconds later, she was back again, bowing, blowing kisses and waving. It was an astonishing thing to see the rapport she had developed with the audience and how she played them until the applause died down and then, off again to the wings.

John looked disturbed at CR's face, which was bright red with enthusiasm, as he continued to clap his hands, then, realizing he was almost the only one left doing so, the big man laughed at himself and wiped his face with a handkerchief.

"Whew. That was exciting!" he said loud enough for the room to hear.

His face began to resume its normal color, which made John relax a bit, not wanting to see the man have a heart attack a few tables away.

"You said she did two performances a night?" Nina asked.

"Yes, but I'm not sure when the next one is," I replied.

The room took on the normal buzz of conversation as Harry Williams took the band through one more number, which I recognized was the song they played just before a break. I was not aware that food was also served in the ballroom and the lull in performance allowed the silverware to resume clattering on the china, glasses to clink in toasting and loud laughter to elevate the noise level.

I took John's hand and asked if he would like to meet Monty and Christa, who were in lively conversation with CR several tables away. As we approached, it seemed discussion that at first appeared lively was in reality an argument about Laura Evans' future.

"You can't mean to parade her around to nightclubs for the rest of her life, can you?" Monty asked. "The girl belongs on the Broadway stage."

"And I suppose you have just the vehicle for her particular talent?" was CR's nasty retort.

"As a matter of fact, I do! We were going to start auditions in a few weeks, and she'd be perfect for the part."

Christa looked perplexed, which made me remember that she had told Miss Manley and me that they didn't have any projects pending due to some backers pulling out at the last minute. She was following the argument as if watching a tennis match looking more confused with each fierce accusation being hurled before standing up as we approached, glad to find an interruption.

"Hello, dear," she said to me, either too flustered to say more or she had forgotten my name. I reminded her and introduced John to her and Monty who had stopped in mid-sentence. He acknowledged our presence but evidently wanted to get back to haggling with CR about who had the better opportunities to present to Lulu.

We made some vague comments about enjoying the evening, looking forward to guests for the weekend and then our conversation fizzled out when the men stopped talking and just glared at each other.

"Well, nice to meet you," John said, taking my elbow and propelling me away from the table that again erupted in loud talk about why CR should bankroll the production Monty had 'in the works' as he put it.

"That doesn't sound like the best method of enticing people to invest with you, does it?" he asked me with a laugh. "They sound like two bull moose in mating season."

"Except one of them is married. No, I hope it is only professional competition with those two. But how silly! Monty doesn't have a production coming up—he told us so. And what does CR know about managing a nightclub singer's career?"

"CR doesn't have to know anything. He'll hire someone to do it."

We had been seated for only a few minutes when the deafening sound of warning bells rang, and we realized it was the fire alarm. We stood quickly, grabbing wraps and purses, looking to leave by the exit to the lobby, but so many people had panicked, standing up abruptly and knocking chairs over in our path. We put those seats upright as we moved forward, the lights in the ballroom flickering to the horrified gasps of guests imagining they would be trapped in the dark while trying to escape a fire. John looked around and pointed to a door off to the side and we ran to it, flung it open and saw that it led directly to the veranda.

"This way!" John called out to the many people pushing their way toward the lobby.

"Do you smell smoke?" Nina asked from directly behind me.

"No, but it could be a fire in the upper floors somewhere."

We took deep breaths of the cool evening air and moved quickly onto the front lawns of the hotel where people were already gathered, looking back at the large building lit up by its flickering electric lights.

I put on my shawl and stood with the others watching guests continue to pour out through the door we had found as well as through the lobby, interspersed with hotel staff, chefs, waiters, maids and housekeepers.

"Is there even a fire brigade somewhere near?" I asked, using that odd terminology because I couldn't imagine an actual fire department closer than Pittsfield, which was some distance away.

John and the reverend looked at each other and evidently decided they could be of some help by returning inside the building despite Nina's and my protests to wait outside. We realized it was futile. They would have to participate in evacuating the building and helping any incapacitated people.

The alarm suddenly stopped and the lights in the building were now stabilized but shining so brightly it was hard to make out other faces in the darker area on the lawn. Did Monty and Christa make it out? What about CR? Was anybody still in the building? We were milling about talking with our eyes on the wide-open double front doors when CR came out and held his hands up to quiet the crowd.

The Fosters, father and son, quickly moved in front of him and Foster Senior addressed everyone.

"We think everything is all right. There does not seem to be any fire or smoke. Perhaps a malfunction of the alarm system. Some of my staff are going room to room to make sure everyone has made it out and that everything is safe. Thank you for your patience." The three men went back inside.

Nina and I looked at each other wondering what we were expected to do now. Other patrons who were not hotel guests evidently took the opportunity to get their cars and slowly drive away leaving a smaller group of guests and staff still standing on the lawn. I saw Lester leaning next to his bass against a large tree, the other musicians nearby smoking and Harry walking up to them and chatting. It must have been close to another half-hour before the Sheriff's car came swiftly down into the shallow valley, stopped in front of the building and four men barreled out onto the front steps and into the building. A short while later another car approached, which turned out to be Bernard and Sophia coming back from Hartford.

She looked alarmed but, of course, said nothing, scanning the crowd for Lulu.

Bernard saw us and asked what was going on. We explained as best we could that we had no idea if there was a fire of any kind, just that the alarm sounded and everyone left the building and that the Fosters and CR were inside checking rooms, as were John and the reverend. Bernard turned off the ignition and as he started to get out of the driver's side, Sophia put her hand on his arm as if to hold him back from danger. He pulled away and trotted up the stairs.

It was a long while before the reverend and John came out and we breathed a sigh of relief to know that they were fine with no hint of smoke about them.

"CR thinks someone pulled the alarm," John said. "There's nobody left in the building except the Sheriff and his men, CR and two staff people."

"And Bernard," I added.

"Didn't see him."

Some minutes later CR came out the front doors, put his hands out as if to quell a mob rather than the perplexed group who stood before him.

"There is nothing to worry about. It was a malfunction with the fire alarm," he said with a smile.

"Why did he say that?" I asked. "You would think it would be more reassuring to know the alarm was pulled by accident rather than safety equipment isn't working properly.

John shrugged. "Enough excitement for one night. Let's get home."

Chapter 8

It was a desultory ride back through the dark toward West Adams, our bright evening extinguished by that bizarre incident. Who would do such a thing? Who wanted to sabotage the Mountain Aire's success? A disgruntled guest? Ridiculous. Surely not the sellers, the Foster family, since that would be a losing bargaining point in the sale that the safety system in the building was faulty. I couldn't imagine that it was someone's idea of a joke. I looked back at Nina and the reverend subdued in the back seat. The idea struck me that Roger had been guilty of what he considered a prank telephone call not too long ago but then remembered he was not working that evening so could not have been the one to pull the alarm. That is not to say that he wasn't at the hotel.

Nina sighed loudly. "We were having such a lovely time."

John looked at her in the rearview mirror. "There will be another time, I'm sure."

"I guess you'll just have to revert to your reverend status for a while still," she said to her husband, who smiled tenderly in return.

As we slowed down to approach their house, I noticed lights on in Miss Manley's house and Stuart's car in the driveway; I had forgotten about their arrival in all the recent turmoil.

"Although it's late, perhaps we all better go inside and greet Stuart and Glenda before calling it a night," I said. John looked at his watch hoping to be spared the interaction, but the Lewises seemed to be pleased with the suggestion, so we all trudged across the back lawn and in through the French windows to the sitting room where the three of them looked up at our approach. I always felt strange about going into someone's home without announcing myself, but it was my home now, too, and Miss Manley was not surprised to see us and, putting her knitting down, stood up to greet us.

"Look at you! What an evening you must have had to come back so late."

I embraced Glenda, who was developing a bit of a tummy, then shook Stuart's hand.

"It was *quite* an evening," the reverend said to Miss Manley's gesture to sit down.

Glenda excused herself briefly, returning shortly with a tray with glasses and the bottle of gin I had requested. "I have the feeling we are going to hear an exciting story," she said.

As I well knew, neither Glenda nor Stuart needed a drink to listen to an exciting story but none of us objected, least of all Miss Manley, who could tell from the reverend's deep breath before beginning that it was going to be a good one.

Two drinks apiece and sometime later, when the reverend wrapped up his retelling of events, we were exhausted but no less out of suppositions as to what had transpired at the hotel, although Stuart seemed more impressed about Cash Ridley and Montgomery Davis being in the narrative.

He pushed his blond hair off his forehead and leaned forward. "You know, of course, that having a fire and collecting the insurance money is one of the oldest tricks in the book."

"But there wasn't a fire," Miss Manley said. "Was there?"

"No," Reverend Lewis answered. "No smoke. No fire. No damage."

"At least not to the physical building but who knows what reputational harm was inflicted?"

"And think of all those who came for dinner and a show and left without paying," I added in my usual practical way.

"Cui bono?" Stuart said, holding up a finger for emphasis. "Who benefits?"

"If the Foster family owns the hotel, why did Mr. Ridley try to take charge of things?" Glenda asked.

"I thought he intended to buy the hotel, isn't that what you said, John?" I asked. I was aware that Stuart and Glenda were not aware of the familiarity between us until that moment.

"That's what someone told me, but perhaps the transfer wasn't finalized."

"Who told you?" Stuart asked.

"I'd rather not say," was John's reply, ever conscious of confidentiality, which received a scoffing sound from Stuart.

"Could it have been an accident?" Glenda asked and we all turned to her. "I mean, perhaps someone stumbled and grabbed at the wall and pulled the alarm by mistake."

"I, for one, am very tired. If you'll excuse me, goodnight, everyone," John said, and I walked with him out the French doors far enough into the garden so the women inside wouldn't see him kiss me goodnight.

"Dear Glenda is such a birdbrain sometimes," he said, laughing. "It's getting chilly—you'd better get back inside before Sherlock Holmes and Watson solve the mystery without you." I watched him leave, then went back inside.

I was exhausted by the long day, the excitement of the evening and the long dissection of events and motivations of all involved, not to mention the two drinks, so I excused myself and looked forward to sleeping in Saturday morning.

Chapter 9

What I imagined was to be a lazy morning started off with the telephone ringing many times before Annie answered it, then her trying to quietly mount the stairs and having to pound on Stuart and Glenda's door before they awoke to the news that there was an urgent call from New York. Stuart grumbled and muttered and with his typical heavy tread made his way downstairs to the telephone located just inside the kitchen. Rather than closing the door, he carried on a loud conversation consisting mostly of saying, "What?" and "How did that happen?" "And then what happened?"

All right, I was now thoroughly awake and was not going to be able to go back to sleep. I was exiting the bathroom when Stuart grumbled his way upstairs and either didn't see me or preferred to ignore me standing there. He slammed the door to his room and began a loud conversation with Glenda that involved calling someone else a nincompoop, accompanied by what must have been his suitcase dragged out of the closet to be packed.

I dressed and met Miss Manley on the landing as we heard the back door slam shut and an animated conversation between Annie and Elsie, Reverend Lewis's maid.

The telephone rang again, and John told me the distressing news about Highfields and that I was to accompany him. I ran upstairs to get a cardigan and my purse, nearly colliding with Stuart, who was wrestling a suitcase down the stairs, Glenda at his back, tugging closed the belt of her bathrobe.

"I've got to get back to the City," was all that Stuart said.

I looked inquiringly at Glenda.

"There is some crisis at the company," she said. It appeared that he was going back by himself, leaving Glenda here, but I didn't have time to ask questions, grabbed my sweater and purse and trotted back to the kitchen.

"What a commotion!" Miss Manley said as both Stuart and I flew through the kitchen, me grabbing a piece of toast as he took a sausage.

"Got to go!" he said, planting a kiss on his aunt's cheek and making for the driveway.

I was hungry, turned around and took another piece of toast with an apology to Annie, and sprinted across the back garden, through the passage between Miss Manley's and the Lewises' houses and out to the back of Doctor Taylor's home and office. He had just shut the office door and walked quickly to the car, opened the passenger side for me and got in behind the wheel.

"Morning," he said.

"What a morning," I responded.

We pulled out to Main Street several hundred yards behind Stuart's unmistakably flashy car and John looked at me inquiringly.

"Some to-do at the publishing house, I think," I said. "Lots of shouting on the telephone, grumbling, stomping, then a swift getaway to Manhattan."

"Hmm," John said, likely thinking it was no great loss.

"What do we know so far?"

"Girl on the front step is all Officer Reed said."

"How odd."

We drove faster than usual along the central street in West Adams since it was early on a Saturday morning and very few people were up and about, down the road and took a right at the fork up toward Highfields.

A group of people including Officer Reed stood on the porch behind the set of steps with a sheet covering what I assumed to be a body, and they looked expectantly as John and I drove up and around the circular drive. Monty Davis, wearing a bathrobe over pajamas, skirted the object on the steps and shuffled in his leather bedroom slippers over to where we parked the car.

"Thank God!" he said in his rich baritone. Over his shoulder, still standing on the porch, was Christa, also in bathrobe and slippers, her hair in some kind of net covering pin curls, and oddly, the maid, Alice, fully dressed in uniform calmly by her side.

"Alice, were you the one to find the body?"

"Oh, no, sir. It was Tillie, but she went to pieces right away. She came out to get the newspaper and ran screaming back into the house. We came out from the kitchen and thought she said, 'Buddy outside' although we don't know anyone named Buddy. She just kept screaming and shaking so the cook and I came out to look and saw this poor girl lying on the steps, very still. Cook was much braver than I was and put her hand over the girl's heart for some moments and declared that she was dead. Terrible! Such a lovely young girl. I went into the house and got a sheet to cover her while Cook called the police."

John stepped forward and with his back to me lifted the sheet and extended his hand to check for a pulse. His broad back blocked my view and my curiosity was aroused. Who was she? What was she doing here?

John shook his head and addressed Christa, who had her hand to her mouth. "Do you recognize her?"

Monty gave a vociferous, "Certainly not!" but Christa only shook her head as if incapable of speech.

John replaced the sheet.

"Why don't you go back inside," John said to the couple, and after they left, he addressed Alice. "Can you get two men to help me move her inside?"

The maid looked distressed, nodded and went inside, as well.

"Do you suppose it's that young girl who disappeared last week?" I asked.

"Who?" John and Reed asked simultaneously.

"Miss Manley's tea group was talking about it. Mona something-or-other. A teenager who wanted to run away to New York."

They both shook their heads, whether to indicate not having heard of it or not knowing who the young girl I was referring to was.

The gardener and the chauffeur came from the side yard of the house and approached tentatively, having heard of the event but probably not imagining they would be called into service. They looked at one another, then the doctor and Officer Reed, and seemed perplexed.

"Should we just carry her like this?" the gardener asked.

"You can't very well put her in a wheelbarrow, can you?" Reed said.

The two men nodded and approached, one to what must have been the shoulders under the sheet and the other under her knees. As they lifted, the cloth slipped away from the face as did some of the blood-matted hair, and I gasped.

It was Lulu Evans.

Chapter 10

At my sharp intake of breath, the two men nearly stumbled and might have dropped her on the steps if John hadn't put a steadying hand on the gardener's arm. I hadn't seen him at Highfields before so he may not have been familiar with the previous death—but who expects to encounter a dead body on any given day? Especially one as gruesome looking as this, one side of her temple smashed in and quite a lot of blood in her hair and on her clothes.

Alice motioned us toward the morning room near the front entrance, the place where Inspector Gladstone had grilled us after the death of Judge Nash. There was a small table with chairs in the middle of the room, a desk facing the bay window and a sofa opposite where she was gently placed before they quickly left.

"You recognized her," I said.

John nodded his head and I wondered why Monty and Christa had not. He did a very cursory external exam, feeling around the back of her head for any injury, but we could both see the obvious fracture of the skull on one side and a bruise on the other side as if she had been hit and then struck her head.

"Poor girl," I said.

There was a howl from another room nearby and Alice came back and said Miss Champion was in a bad way. John re-covered the body, asked the maid to stay for a few minutes and we followed the sounds of loud weeping from the living room where Christa was hysterical, actually pulling at her hair while seated on the sofa.

"Pull yourself together!" Monty said to her, shaking her by the shoulders. Then he slapped her across the face, and she toppled to the side and whimpered instead.

"Really, sir! We don't treat agitation in that way anymore." John looked sternly at Monty, who clearly was not expecting anyone to have witnessed the blow, then he approached Christa and pulled her to a more upright position and looked into her eyes.

"Has she taken some kind of narcotics?" John asked. I leaned over and noticed that her pupils were rather large in spite of there being an abundance of natural light in the room.

Monty stammered. "Yes...uh...I gave her something a little while ago."

John glowered at him. "Well?"

Monty dug in the pocket of his bathrobe and pulled out a pill bottle and handed it to the doctor.

"How many?"

"Just one."

John turned the bottle around to look more closely at the label. "This prescription is made out to you."

"Yes, that's right." Monty was starting to get some of his bravado back.

"Did it occur to you that your doctor made the dosage based upon your size and weight? And not that of a petite woman?"

Monty stared open-mouthed, speechless possibly for the first time.

"It is very dangerous to medicate other people, even if it is your spouse. This is a high dosage, and you can clearly see that she is feeling the effects strongly."

"I'm sorry, darling," Monty said, sitting down beside his wife and putting his arm around her. "But at least she is not having hysterics anymore." He continued to pat her shoulder.

I thought John was going to do something rash himself, so I suggested we relieve Alice of her duty in the morning room and practically dragged him out by the arm to avoid what I surely thought might be a confrontation.

"That man is an ass! She could have had an overdose. He'd better be telling the truth about it being only one pill or we'll have another emergency on our hands," John said.

"I've called for Inspector Gladstone from Pittsfield to come," Officer Reed said, standing at the door. He had probably done so more to protect himself from blame if some protocol was not followed rather than needing the assistance of the cranky inspector who, from my past experience dealing with him, acted as if everyone was a suspect.

We three returned to the morning room and saw Alice was more than happy to be relieved of her duty next to Lulu. As she passed me, she asked if I would like a cup of coffee with her in the kitchen.

"That would be lovely, let me just tell the doctor."

She disappeared down the hall to the back of the house with me following just a few moments later.

As I passed the large sitting room, Monty grabbed me by the arm and pulled me into the doorway of the room. He had changed from a concerned husband to a monster within minutes.

"Don't you *dare* breathe a word of what you just saw, understood?"

He pushed me back into the hallway, and, stunned, I staggered into the kitchen at the far end of the house and sat on one of the stools by a large butcher block slab in the middle of the room. I didn't know if I was more angry or frightened.

Alice turned around and stopped her coffee preparations to look at me more closely.

"Are you all right?"

I gathered my wits about me and managed a wan smile. "Yes, fine. Interesting household here."

She turned back to the stove and spoke over her shoulder. "You don't know the half of it." She adjusted the heat under the percolator and sat opposite me. "At first, we were told they were theater people, so I had the idea we would have a house full of acrobats or jugglers." She laughed and covered her mouth with dainty hands. "Imagine my surprise when they came up the driveway in that expensive car and stepped out as if they were Mr. and Mrs. John D. Rockefeller, dressed in furs, both of them, the height of summer if you can believe it. Mr. Davis saw us all staring at them, and he lashed out right away at Edna, the new girl and the first person he saw, and it's been like that ever since. His wife is nice, but every conversation they have is so dramatic with loud voices and tears."

The coffee was percolating, and Alice stood to keep a better eye on it. She also checked the doorway in the event someone might intrude on our conversation.

"And the telephone rings at all hours of the day and night! I hope they have stock in Bell Telephone because they must spend a fortune on calls. Mr. Davis actually yells and screams on the phone at people. And the language! I may look for another job soon. It's too difficult here."

She turned off the burner and got out cups, saucers and a small plate of cookies. "I think your job seems swell. How do you become a nurse?"

I was looking forward to the coffee to make up for the lack of breakfast earlier—if you didn't count the two pieces of toast I swiped—and I told her about applying for nursing school, the training and that it suited me well.

"As long as you can tolerate the sight of blood," I added. "One student fainted the first day of class and the Head Nurse was merciless to her after that."

"Oh, I've seen enough blood, all right. The men in our family are hunters and I've dressed my share of animals. I'm more worried about affording the cost of training. Well, we'll see."

We finished our short break and she put cups and saucers on a tray and brought them to where the others had adjourned to the sitting room, with neither Monty nor Christa in sight. As an afterthought, she had added another set for Inspector Gladstone, but the small, grim man had already arrived and put himself in the morning room. As before, he kept his hat on in the house and looked at me with a twist of his mouth when I put my head around the door to see if Lulu's body was still undisturbed.

"Well, well. Fancy *you* being here."

"In my professional capacity. I am Doctor Taylor's nurse," I clarified in a haughty tone because I wasn't in uniform that day.

He either snorted or huffed in return, but I wasn't going to be cowed by him.

I thought it disrespectful for us to be talking while poor Lulu's body lay on the sofa and made no hesitation in saying so.

Then I added, "The funeral director's people from Adams have been called and are coming shortly."

"Did you know the deceased?"

"I met her before at the Mountain Aire Hotel where she was performing."

He motioned me to sit down. I remained standing.

"And were you well acquainted?"

"As I said, Inspector, I met her at the hotel. The band leader introduced us when I was there earlier this week. Other than that, I only saw her perform."

He wrote in a notebook he pulled out of his pocket, paused and scribbled more. He smiled but it was more like a grimace. "I've heard of that place. What sort of performing did she do?" He made it sound as if she were an exotic dancer.

"She was the featured singer with the band. Popular songs, you know." I left it at that, almost certain he would next ask me which songs those were.

"Was she acquainted with the people who live here?" he asked.

I was getting more annoyed with him by the moment. "I suppose that is something that you should ask them. Now, if you'll excuse me," I said, returning to the sitting room down the hall, my temper rising with each step. Both John and Officer Reed turned at my entrance but remained looking at me, probably because steam was coming out of my ears.

"Coffee?" John offered.

"Thank you," I replied graciously, and they both sensed it was better not to engage me in conversation just then.

Inspector Gladstone appeared at the door of the sitting room. "What the devil!" he said, surveying what must have looked like a cozy mid-morning coffee break. Officer Reed jumped to his feet, his full face reddening. "If you could get what's-her-name, the maid."

"Alice," Reed said.

"To get those people…"

"Mr. and Mrs. Davis," Reed supplied.

"Yes, them!"

"She told me that they were getting dressed," Reed said. He fiddled with the napkin in his hand.

"This is not a garden party! What do you mean, getting dressed?" Gladstone was shouting by now and he pushed his hat further back on his head, uncovering the wiry hair sticking up.

"They were in their nightclothes," Reed said.

Gladstone glared at each of us in turn as if we had something to do with their attire.

The doorbell rang, giving him the opportunity to save face. "That will be the funeral home people, I expect," and he left the room.

John looked at me and raised his eyebrows. "I'd better see that they don't disturb the body more than necessary." He left, followed by Officer Reed. I had the room to myself and remembered how Mrs. Nash had wanted to—or was persuaded to—redecorate this room into some Art Deco showpiece, which was all the rage just then, but would have utterly ruined the quasi-rustic feel of the place. In its present state, it could be considered a little old-fashioned but, in spite of one decorator's opinion that it was dark and gloomy, it was actually well-lit with a dazzling view of Mount Greylock, the local landmark of note. More of a hill to somebody well-traveled, but its height was not the prominent feature; rather it was the aspect viewed from the house. It would be lovely to sit here and watch the progress of the sun across the carpeting inside and the lawns outside. My reverie was broken by Monty Davis's entering the room by himself.

He was neatly dressed and freshly groomed, with a huge smile on his face as if there hadn't been a body found on his front doorstep and he hadn't threatened me not so long ago. I did not return the smile and resumed looking out the windows.

"Gorgeous view, isn't it?" he said as if nothing unpleasant had occurred.

Alice came into the room and announced that Inspector Gladstone wished to speak with him. Monty put on a concerned face and solemnly followed her into the morning room. I went to the hall to see a stretcher borne by two men taking Lulu's body out toward the front door, John watching them in their progress. He turned, saw me and suggested that we check in with Christa, who he had been told "was not feeling well."

Alice led us upstairs to the bedroom although we knew the way already and let us into the same suite that Mrs. Nash had used, with all of its furniture and decorations intact. Christa lay flat on her back, still in nightgown and bathrobe, snoring lightly in a state my younger brother would have described as 'passed out.'

"I was worried she might not be breathing from what he gave her," John said, approaching the bed and lifting an eyelid, then checking her pulse. "But she seems okay. She'll just have to sleep it off. Inspector Gladstone won't be happy."

"I don't think Inspector Gladstone has had a happy day in all his life."

Chapter 11

John dropped me in West Adams while he went on to the funeral home in Adams to do a more complete examination of Lulu, short of an actual autopsy to be performed by a doctor in Pittsfield. I dragged myself into Miss Manley's kitchen feeling as though it was late in the day instead of closer to noon. Annie looked at me anxiously.

"Was it bad?"

I sighed in response. "I don't know how to answer that question. It was Lulu Evans from the Mountain Aire Hotel—a very young girl. Hit in the head, it looks like."

That produced a gasp from Annie.

"It was probably quick. But lots of blood. Head wound, you know." Somehow my comments seemed shallow and unfeeling.

"What was she doing up at Highfields?"

I shrugged.

Miss Manley came into the room. "Oh, dear. Would you like something to eat?"

It was such a strange thing to have asked and such an awful morning that I almost laughed aloud at the absurdity.

"I'd like to lie down for a bit," I said, suddenly bone-weary. I pulled myself upstairs by the banister, sat on the bed and was asleep moments after my shoes were off. I must have slept a long time, waking with a groggy feeling and confirming my extended nap by looking at my watch. And now I was hungry.

Miss Manley and Glenda were in the sitting room with the French windows open to the sunny garden. Glenda stood up as soon as I came into the room.

"We wanted to stay inside in case you needed anything. I've never known you to sleep so long," she said.

"Please, sit down. Let me get my bearings before I go to the kitchen and eat half a chicken or something."

Miss Manley smiled gently. "Glenda, why don't you tell Aggie about why you are still here."

"Oh, sure. In all the commotion this morning I suppose we didn't communicate what was going on. Charlie, you know, Stuart's partner, hired a college boy to help out this summer as they are gearing up for the release of some series for young men. The idea was that *maybe* we could have a bit of a vacation before the baby comes."

She was many months away from that event, which made me wonder if she was fully prepared for the actuality of the total immersion involved in bringing up a child. I might have said something if it were just the two of us but decided not to with Miss Manley present.

"That's why we thought we could come up for the weekend. Charlie is out of town and Frank was supposed to pick up the galleys yesterday and somehow couldn't find the printing plant in Brooklyn. He said he had never been to Brooklyn before and spent ten dollars on a cab, riding around before giving up."

"Is Brooklyn so difficult to navigate?" Miss Manley asked.

"I don't know. I've never been there either," Glenda responded.

"Yes, you have. Remember when we went to Coney Island? That's in Brooklyn. But I also went to Sonia Berman's home in Crown Heights once for dinner. It was a Friday night Seder and she thought I might enjoy it."

"Oh," said Glenda in a tone that implied she hadn't been invited.

"It took a long time from Manhattan only because the subway made so many stops and then we had to change lines. The ride to Coney Island is direct and you and I were having such a good time, you probably didn't notice that it was almost an hour. But if you look at a map, it really isn't so far from the city."

"My goodness," Miss Manley said, clicking away on her knitting needles. "You girls are fearless!"

"Now remember, Miss Manley, you were the one who went to Europe without your parents at a much younger age."

82

She smiled at the memory. "That's true. But we were not only watched like hawks for misbehavior, but we also felt very protected."

I looked up to see John coming across the back garden without his hat or bag and, seeing us through the open French window, he knocked lightly on the jamb and smiled before being welcomed in.

"Glenda, you are looking well."

"Thank you," she said, pleased with the compliment.

Before anyone could ask him to sit down, he asked to speak with me. Clearly in private.

"Miss Manley, would you mind if we commandeer the kitchen for a bit. I still haven't had lunch; why don't you join me?" I asked him.

Evidently, he hadn't had lunch, either, having just come from the funeral home in

Adams. Annie muttered something about an errand and left us alone. I poured him a glass of milk and set about to slice some ham to make sandwiches for us both. He was quiet while I worked, and he waited until I had finished and presented the plates in front of us. He closed the door to the kitchen and retook his seat.

"It's clear that she died from that head wound, as we suspected," he said.

"Poor thing. She was so young."

John nodded, a crease forming between his eyebrows. "Something is not right about the whole thing. She obviously died early last night, and it seems strange that she was not discovered until this morning."

"Do you think she was killed before or after the Davises got back from the Mountain Aire?"

"That's the dilemma, isn't it? Doctor Carter and I couldn't be more specific about the exact time of death, but if she were killed before they got back, why didn't they see her on their front step?"

"Maybe the chauffeur drove them around to the back of the house. Or maybe she was killed after they returned," I suggested. I took another bite of the sandwich, and a thought suddenly came to me. "There was a lot of confusion last night and with the lights flickering on and off it was difficult to see who was out on the lawn and who left by car. Perhaps Lulu went back with Monty and Christa."

"Why would she do that? She was provided a room at the hotel."

"I didn't know that. But she wouldn't have been able to get to her room right away anyway."

John shook his head. "That doesn't make sense. She was still in her performance clothes."

We ate in silence while I tried to make sense of what she was doing at Highfields.

"The worst part of my day was Sophia coming to identify Lulu's body."

I inhaled sharply, imagining the dreadful scene.

"Bernard had driven the poor woman to see the specialist in Hartford yesterday and they didn't get back until things calmed down. Evidently, Harry Williams was crushed that the audience had just up and left on what should have been a spectacularly successful evening, so he said he didn't bother looking for Lulu— figured she was upset with the interrupted performance. It seems nobody looked for her until it got very late, and Sophia began to worry about her. Not too much, as it seems Lulu often stayed out late. When she woke up this morning, went to her cousin's room and saw she was not there, she thought the worst, that Lulu had spent the night with someone. Then she learned that was not the worst."

"She was able to speak to tell you all that?"

John looked critically at me. "Partially. Bernard came with her, and he filled in the bits that she was not able to relay in her croaking whisper. She was totally bereft and guilty about not having done something sooner."

I shook my head in sympathy. "What an appalling situation." I toyed with the fork at my place setting.

"You know all those poems and references about roses?" he asked, his eyes getting misty.

84

I didn't know where he was going with this and let him continue.

"'Gather ye rosebuds' and you know, all the symbolic references to the fleeting nature of life using roses as a metaphor."

I extended my hand to his across the table, moved by his emotion but couldn't help asking, "Why do you say roses?"

He looked startled. "Because there were rose petals in her hair. You remember she wore flowers in her hair when she performed. All that was left were some stray petals."

"She wore a gardenia in her hair," I said.

John pulled his hand away. "Must you be so literal at a time like this?"

"I'm sorry, but they are two very different flowers. And that could make quite an important difference."

He gave me a hard look, reached into his jacket pocket and pulled out a piece of paper, carefully unfolded it and showed me two small, yellow petals.

"Those are rose petals. Gardenias are generally white and heavily scented." I sniffed and came away with a faint odor of rose and offered it back to him for verification. He inhaled once, twice, said nothing, left the packet on the table and stood up.

"Thank you for lunch. It's been a long day already and I for one am very tired. I'll talk to Officer Reed and Inspector Gladstone about your analysis. And I'll see you on Monday."

No sooner had he left out the back door than Glenda poked her head around the corner.

"I certainly hope you weren't listening to our conversation," I said sharply.

"Trouble in paradise?" she asked with what was meant to be a coy smile.

I glared at her, picked up the two plates and brought them to the sink.

"Aggie, I'm sorry. I wasn't eavesdropping, I was just coming into the kitchen to get a glass of milk and heard what seemed to be an uncharacteristically strong tone."

"Not at all," I said, daring her to admit that she had overheard the specifics of our talk.

She sidled up next to me, a familiar wheedling technique she had, while I washed and rinsed the two plates and did not respond.

"I had a good idea for what to do this afternoon. I know it's getting toward the end of the season, but let's go blueberry picking."

I had never heard her suggest a rustic outdoor adventure, but the lure of being outside and away was just the tonic I needed after a long workweek and an emotionally difficult day.

"Do you know of any good places?"

"Aggie! You may think I am a creature of urban areas and interior places, but I was once a little girl with a fondness for blueberry muffins. My mother and I used to go out each August and get enough for muffins and a pie at least once a week."

"That sounds wonderful," I said, just thinking of the fresh fruits that were so hard to come by in New York City and the suburbs and expensive, to boot. "I could stand to get some fresh air."

Glenda turned to pick up the remaining utensils and glasses from the table and saw the packet that John had left.

"What's this?"

Before I could answer, she had already unfolded the paper and looked at the two petals enclosed within.

"These are from my mother's climbing rose bush by the front door," she said.

Chapter 12

Not long after, John came back to the kitchen and beckoned me to follow him. We walked to his car, he held open the passenger door and said, "Let's go up to Highfields."

We didn't talk on the drive up and he slowed down as we approached the house and looked intently at the front door area.

"What is it?" I asked.

"I don't see anything resembling roses, do you?"

He drove slowly on the driveway to the back of the house, scrutinizing the landscaping and shaking his head.

"Something doesn't add up," he said. "Although Lulu was found on her back, the body's lividity suggests otherwise. She was moved after death to this place is my guess."

"From where?" As I asked the question, I had an answer. "Let's go back to town."

He pulled up in his driveway and I led the way to Glenda's house. It didn't take long for him to ascertain that the origin of the rose petals came from the pale-yellow climber that arched itself over the front door.

"I'd better call Inspector Gladstone," John said wearily, going back to his house while I returned to Miss Manley's and accompanied Glenda into the kitchen for a glass of lemonade. I was bursting with the news about the rose petals and John's information about Lulu's body being moved but was interrupted by Officer Reed looking for Annie, who was off on an errand in town. He always looked a little flushed, probably from the heavy uniform he wore, so I invited him to sit down and have a glass of buttermilk, a sure-fire cooling drink. A few minutes later, Annie returned with the *Berkshire Eagle* tucked under her arm and a packet of peaches from the greengrocer. I knew that there would be a conversation about ongoing events at Highfields, and there was no way I was going to miss it.

Without prompting, Reed launched into mild grievances about the Davis household's reluctance to provide any information about whether either Monty or Christa or any of the staff knew Lulu Evans.

"Monty and Christa saw her perform at the Mountain Aire last night and they had mentioned they had seen her perform before," I said.

"He might have met her before that," Annie said. "Wouldn't an aspiring actress know about Monty Davis living at Highfields?"

"How do you know she was an aspiring actress?" Reed asked with surprise.

"It stands to reason. She was a singer, and I heard the only reason she got her big chance to perform up here was that her cousin lost her voice. Everyone says she was very popular, and the men couldn't stop talking about her. Surely she was hoping for something bigger."

Reed raised his eyebrows in skepticism but said nothing. Like me, he was probably wondering where Annie got her information. I smiled inwardly, imagining her having a secret subscription to *Variety.*

"That's not an unreasonable assumption," Glenda said. "In New York show business you've got to have irons in every fire."

"There was some loud conversation at the table with Cash Ridley and Monty where they were both extolling her talents and where she could best be used. CR, as he likes people to call him, said he was ready to bankroll a nightclub debut in Manhattan while Monty was talking about casting her in a new production. In some ways, it seemed more about the ego of the two men than anything else," I said.

"I can't imagine his wife was too pleased to hear her husband go on about Lulu. She missed out on a good role recently and he might have been looking to replace her," Annie said as she put the peaches in a bowl.

"How in the world do you know that?" Reed asked, turning to look at her.

"Oh, I hear things," she said dismissively.

"That hardly gives Monty a motive to kill Lulu. In fact, quite the opposite. He would want to protect the goose that laid the golden egg," Glenda said.

"What about his wife?" Annie asked.

Reed's head swiveled following our conversation.

"If Lulu was the golden egg, Christa would benefit financially, too. It would not be in her long-term interests to get rid of her," I commented.

"Unless she was insanely jealous."

"I have an idea that they have a more tolerant marriage than that," I said.

Officer Reed stood up. "I'd better be going," he said abruptly, whether shocked at our cold analysis of the situation or worried about revealing something that he knew. As he scraped the chair legs back to get up, Elsie, the Lewises' maid, came in the back door, a bowl in her hand.

"Hello, all. Here to borrow a cup of sugar." She held out the bowl toward Annie, who went into the pantry.

"Afternoon, ladies," Reed said, tipping his hat.

Elsie followed Annie into the pantry. "Well, what do you know?"

"Not much more than we already know," she responded sadly.

I had to laugh. "You two probably know more than Inspector Gladstone and Officer Reed combined! You have quite an efficient intelligence network set up."

Annie waved the comment away. "Just keep my eyes and ears open. Surprising what you can hear."

The back door crashed open, and Roger burst in. "Elsie! I think something's burning in the oven!"

"I hope you turned it off! Thanks, Annie, got to go," and she dashed away.

"Is that lemonade?" Roger asked, looking at the pitcher.

"Do you mean, 'May I have a glass of lemonade?'" Annie prompted.

"Thank you, it looks delicious," and without invitation, he sat down. "I can't believe what happened to Lulu. I'm devastated. We really need to get to the bottom of this." He banged his fist on the table. "What's the poop on the Davis guy?"

"No 'poop' to be had, I'm afraid," Glenda said.

"I'm sorry I was at home last night. Maybe I could have done something to prevent her death."

Glenda put her hand on his shoulder. "It's hard when you're young and it's someone you know. But you can't spend your energy on guilt about it."

"She left the stage after her performance and who knows where she went. Everyone expected her to return at some point for the next set and not too long after the fire alarm went off and it was chaos," I said.

"Was there a fire or was it a false alarm?" He drank down half his glass in one long draught.

"I don't know if there is any new information about why the fire alarm went off since there wasn't any smoke or flames," I said.

"It was a strange evening here with cars coming and going up the street late into the night," Roger said. "Too far from the Aire to have anything to do with it. Probably just Doug having one of his wild parties."

Glenda and I exchanged looks.

"Have you ever been to one of his parties?" she asked.

He squirmed a bit in his seat. "No, I suppose I'm not sophisticated enough to mingle with his crowd." He plopped his head into his hand, looking not only sad about Lulu but dejected about his prospects for the future.

"His crowd? Who does he socialize with in West Adams?" Glenda was genuinely puzzled about which people were included in this group.

"They are his friends from New York who come up. Probably to jeer at us bumpkins. And despite what he said about the 'old goats' getting the girls, he is doing all right for himself."

"If I recall, it was your friend Bobby who made the 'old goats' allusion," I said.

"It doesn't matter. He had women from the City—and male friends, too—but he also had Lulu and Mona a couple of times."

"What!" Glenda said. "Do you know how old she is? What is he thinking? There are laws about that."

"Do you suppose that's where Mona got the notion of running away to New York?" I asked.

"Don't worry. She is safe and sound at home. Locked in her room, I hear," Annie added. It was true that she didn't miss much.

***

Berry picking involved two threats: bears and mosquitoes. The first was unlikely as there had been no sightings recently but we had just a few hours left of daylight without fear of the tiny carnivores. Sturdy shoes, socks, pants, long-sleeved shirts, Citronella oil on the exposed parts and two baskets completed our equipment. There was another threat: eating too many as you went.

Since the prime location was the small valley on the other side of Highfields, we had to take the path up to the house, cross the unmown portion of lawn hugging the trees and back down another lesser-used path to what Glenda called Happy Valley. There were no houses there, just low vegetation and scores of blueberry bushes, and, as it occurred to me it might belong to Highfields, I asked Glenda.

"I don't know who the owner is. My mother and I used to come here, and nobody ever said anything, so I guess it's all right."

That was Glenda: don't ask for permission; rather, wait and apologize later if you need to.

"Isn't this amazing?" she asked.

We set to work, and I was pleased to know that if there were bears in the vicinity, we would surely hear them crashing through the vegetation or see them against the green of the low bushes.

"Aggie, tell me about Lulu's cousin, Sophia."

"She's a beautiful woman who had a marketable singing voice before she damaged her vocal cords." I hesitated, knowing I should not have revealed a patient's medical issues. "It's common knowledge that something happened to her voice. I assume she brought in her cousin to substitute for her under the impression that when she got better, she could resume her position."

"Did you ever see her perform?"

"No."

"Maybe she was worried about Lulu taking her place," Glenda said, popping a berry into her mouth. "By the way, it's not too late in the season; it's just the right time. Mmm."

"Glenda, we do want some for tomorrow morning's muffins." I reached toward the top of the bush, evidently where no human or bear had yet been and found a motherlode. "I don't know what Sophia's performances were like, but you didn't get to see Lulu on stage. Aside from a splendid voice and an attractive exterior, she was just plain sexy."

"Ah, now I see why Roger and the others were crazy about her. You don't think it was a jealous boyfriend? Gosh, it seems like there are so many people who could resent her—her cousin, one of the boys…"

"Oh, surely not one of the boys!"

"As you remember, Roger for one is not as innocent as he pretends."

I put my basket down, not only because it was getting heavy, but I wanted to make a point with her. "Be very careful about what you say or what you are suggesting. It's lucky we are out here with no one in hearing distance rather than back at Miss Manley's where Annie could overhear, spread it about or tell Officer Reed. Besides, Roger was at home last night."

"*So* he said," Glenda said primly.

I let it go and we continued to pick in silence.

"Tell me about this Cash Ridley. He sounds fascinating."

"He's a wealthy New York businessman. I'm surprised Stuart hasn't come into his social circle." It was a catty thing to say, but Stuart was always going on about whom he knew and met and acting surprised that common folk didn't know who his friends were.

"We mostly associate with the literary folks in town, but if this man has funds to invest, you can bet that Stuart will want to meet him."

"His business is about machinery and airplane parts or something."

"That doesn't mean he couldn't be an investor."

"True. He is up here for the summer with a secretary and his former son-in-law, who is his assistant. I guess they just wanted a change of pace from the City. And he is either going to buy or has bought the Mountain Aire."

"The Foster family is selling up? Young George won't be happy with that."

I moved around to the other side of the bush.

She followed me.

"George Foster's son. The hotel has been in the family for two generations at least, the earliest one burned down years ago and somehow they rebuilt. I had the impression that all these new activities there—the band, the singer, the tennis pro—were their attempts at modernization."

"Perhaps they were, and then Cash Ridley comes in and thinks it's a good investment," I said.

Glenda moved closer to where I stood reaching up higher than she could.

"Aggie, you have got to get me to meet this man."

I stopped what I was doing and stared at her. "What exactly is going on with Stuart's business?"

She bit her lip, "There were start-up costs...."

"I thought the Hudson Publishing Company was already established. That was the advantage of entering into that partnership."

Glenda smiled. "Of course, that was a tremendous plus, but they've only been Hudson-Manley a little more than a month. They had to change the names on the door, the stationery, the business cards...."

"That paper and printing must have cost a lot," I noted sarcastically. "You would think perhaps they could have got a break on that considering they are publishers. Miss Manley either gave or loaned you quite a lot of money, not that I am aware of her financial situation, nor it is any of my business."

"Actually, it's *not* any of your business."

"Very well."

"All right."

Conversation came to a halt. We resumed picking blueberries with an eye on the west where the sun had already dipped below the mountains. If we weren't careful, the mosquitoes would be after us soon enough.

"Aggie?"

"Hmm?"

"I'm sorry if I was short with you just now. We aren't broke, you know, and we haven't squandered Miss Manley's money, either. Stuart called it capitalization or something where the funds were used to invest in things that would make the company work more efficiently."

I wondered what Stuart had done with the money and if he had told her the truth, but I realized I didn't want to know.

"Still, Hudson-Manley are always looking for new investors and Cash Ridley sounds like just the kind of person Stuart needs to approach."

"Why doesn't he call and make an appointment?" That seemed the obvious solution to me.

"It would go much more smoothly if he had an introduction of some sort." She blinked her big eyes at me and when I didn't respond, she continued. "Aggie, can't you talk to him?"

"I met him in a professional capacity and then he reciprocated socially, that's all."

"That's enough. Doesn't he have a secretary or something?"

"Well, I have spoken to his assistant several times...."

"That's all it takes." She swatted at her ankle. "The mosquitoes are starting already, and I'll get eaten alive. I think we have enough berries; let's go back."

We turned around toward the path that led up to Highfields, rousing gnats as we walked through the high grass in this wild place.

"I have a great idea," Glenda started, and I tried not to groan aloud at something that would surely involve work on my part. "Why don't we go up to Mountain Aire tomorrow on the pretext of you showing me all the improvements at the site? Or maybe we're just dropping in on Roger or something."

I looked askance at her. "And?"

"Then we casually bump into Mr. Ridley or—what's his assistant's name?"

"Bernard Symington."

"There you go. If we time it during the lunch hour, we're bound to see them near the dining room or the terrace, don't you think?"

"You know Miss Manley will expect us to have Sunday dinner with her tomorrow," I reminded her.

We continued our way upwards toward Highfields and I mistakenly thought she might have given up on the idea.

"All right, here's what we'll do. Tonight, I'll propose that we go up to the hotel for lunch after church. How's that?"

"You're going to church?"

Glenda stuck out her tongue at me. "Yes!"

I had to laugh. What a compromise. "Were you two even married in a church?" I asked.

"No, we went to City Hall instead. No fuss, that's my motto."

"Sure, that's you, all right. No fuss Glenda!" I laughed and ran up the hill as she attempted to chase me but was hampered by the basket and her changing body.

"I'll get you for that remark!" she said, laughing.

Chapter 13

I don't know why Glenda was so averse to attending church, especially because Reverend Lewis was a neighbor and she was close friends with Nina. We had all grown up in the environment of formal church on Sunday and, if you were in an institution such as a private school or, in our case, nursing school, you went to chapel on a daily basis. It was part of the cultural fabric of our lives, although I did wonder about the reaction of girls like our classmate Sonia, who believed in the same God but must have felt awkward when whoever did the reading referred to 'His Son,' along with the Jesus references throughout. We experienced the generic Protestant version of religion in nursing school, and I could tell some of the Catholic students let the words wash over them as familiar terms but probably in their eyes, they were not exactly the right words.

Miss Manley gave very little objection to the proposal of going to the hotel for lunch, which meant that the food for Sunday dinner would serve for Monday evening and beyond. An extra bonus was that Glenda made blueberry muffins that morning while I assisted in the preparation of the rest of breakfast. Miss Manley was delighted by our initiative and even more interested in the break of routine.

Reverend Lewis was a dear man, well educated, interesting and caring deeply about his parishioners. Unfortunately, to be kind, his sermons tended to be on the dry side. His hobby was archaeology and history and there was not a parable in the Bible that didn't bring up some fascinating bit of information, whether it was what the bread was actually like in Jesus's time or what kind of fish might be found in the Sea of Galilee. The geography of the Holy Land was also a passion, and in his study at home the atlas was usually open to the page that depicted Palestine. I had the feeling that if it were possible, he would have had a poster made of that map in order to point out the various locations of events as he spoke. It was an informative sermon, as usual, and not emotive in the least compared to some other branches of the Christian religion, so that the congregation left feeling they had done their duty to their family, community and God and it was not too painful an experience. One saw one's neighbors on the way out of church, had a heavy dinner and perhaps a nap. A good Sunday all around.

Miss Manley and Glenda were both excited to have an outing and to see the hotel in better light and circumstances than the last time. The venue's white painted bricks shone in bright early afternoon sun, the grass was a healthy green, the flowers were in full bloom, eliciting a sigh of delight from both of them as we came around the corner and made the descent into the shallow valley.

"I don't remember the hotel this way growing up," Glenda said. "I guess I wasn't paying much attention the last time we were out here."

"A lot of money and improvements have gone into the transformation, from what I understand," Miss Manley commented.

Glenda parked the car, and we made our way up the front steps, through the lobby and onto the terrace. From this vantage point, we could see the occupants of the swimming pool a ways off, a tennis match in progress and patrons enjoying the fresh air at tables spilling out from the dining room. We walked toward the side of the terrace for a better look at the tennis game and saw Roger attentive at the sidelines, ready to retrieve an out-of-bounds ball. I remembered my two summers working at a girls' day camp in Westchester County and my tennis ability that could have once easily qualified me at a hotel or resort for the position Roger had, if only they had hired girls for such jobs.

We sauntered to the rear lobby entrance and were waved over to the dining area by Bernard, who got up from his table, introduced himself to Miss Manley and Glenda and then invited us to his table, partially shaded by a canvas umbrella. He was seated by himself but clearly anticipated company as there were several empty chairs. We commiserated about the dreadful news of Lulu's death and Bernard seemed truly shaken by it.

"It has been a terrible shock for Sophia, as you can imagine. She and I had just gotten back from Hartford Friday evening to the sight of scores of people on the lawn, all looking back at the hotel. We couldn't make sense of it but managed to edge into the crowd and several guests told us what they knew, which wasn't much. Sophia, of course, was looking for Lulu, but it was impossible to make out individual faces in the mass of people milling about so she waited until the all-clear was announced and went back to her own room, not suspecting a thing."

"It was chaotic but there turned out to be no reason to be afraid for her," I said. "Lulu could just as easily have been outside among the crowd or perhaps she had a date." That sounded flimsy even to me since I knew that she had been expected to perform another set that evening.

"Imagine Sophia's guilt yesterday when she woke to find that her cousin hadn't come back, and she hadn't raised the alarm about it," Bernard said.

"She couldn't have suspected or known anything was the matter," Miss Manley said, patting him on the hand. It was the first indication I had that there might have been some affection between Bernard and Sophia, though it took Miss Manley to pick up on the signals.

He stood up as Cash Ridley and Catherine approached the table. CR had aged considerably since I saw him Friday night and the ebullient façade had been replaced by an almost un-recognizable somber character. He nodded to me, and introductions went around the table before a waiter hustled up to give us menus. CR put his hand on his place setting and sighed.

"What an awful, terrible thing to lose a young life like that," he said.

We nodded and murmured our condolences and I wished we hadn't come at all. Glenda had made his acquaintance, at least an introduction, and I felt it was time to leave him with his grief. I looked at Miss Manley for guidance and thought she might politely excuse us all, but I was once again surprised by her perceptiveness.

"Mr. Ridley, I feel you might want to be left alone but I can assure you, it will be better if you suffer through our company and idle chatter. It will be one more meal that you got through, and by tomorrow, one more day will have passed. It's difficult, but what options do we humans have?"

He smiled ruefully at her and nodded. "Yes, I've suffered losses before and I know I will survive this one, too."

"If you don't mind, I would very much like to hear about your business interests in New York," Miss Manley said, tipping her head to one side in that birdlike way she had.

He started slowly; then seeing he had the interest of us all, he began to talk about how he started his company, the obstacles he faced, how he conquered them, and where he hoped to take it into the future. It was a long conversation that lasted most of the meal and it seemed to cheer him up to relate his successes and past endeavors.

I glanced over at Catherine, who must have heard this recitation many times, but she listened politely, nodding her head at the appropriate times. This must have been a familiar narrative for Bernard, too, but he didn't seem to be listening. His attention was riveted on someone on the other side of the terrace. Miss Manley and I both turned our heads to see what had caught his eye, but only saw guests seated at tables and a female staff member serving them. Bernard noticed that we had followed his glance and he abruptly cleared his throat, which drew our gaze back to him, and he smiled.

"Thought I saw someone I used to know."

***

We were quiet on the way back home after the melancholy tone of lunch with Cash Ridley trying desperately to appear that everything was normal while I suspected some vital part of his earlier exuberant character had been dulled forever by Lulu's death. It was a horrible and sad event on all fronts.

Glenda parked the car and we trudged back to the house, taking off our hats and gloves in the warming afternoon, and I looked forward to sitting outside and reading while Miss Manley might get on with her most recent knitting project, a tiny sweater for her soon-to-be grandnephew or -niece. We had only just entered the back door when the telephone rang, an unusual thing on a Sunday in West Adams.

"For you," Glenda said, holding the earpiece out to Miss Manley.

It may have been impolite of us not to move away, but we were mesmerized by hearing a woman's overwrought voice on the other end while Miss Manley tried her most soothing tone.

"We'll be right there."

She hung up the earpiece, plopped her black peach basket hat back on her head, tugged on her gloves, and said to me, "Would you drive me to see Christa? She is very upset."

"I can drive you," Glenda offered, not wishing to be left out of whatever drama was transpiring at Highfields.

"No, dear. I think it would not be a good idea in your condition. Besides, you haven't met Christa yet, and under the circumstances she might think it a bit of an intrusion."

"Very well," Glenda said, handing me the car key. She gave me a look that I interpreted to mean, *you'd better fill me in on every detail when you get back.*

"Don't you think I should stay here, too?" I asked, not wanting to seem too forward.

"Aggie, she knows you personally as well as professionally. I think it is appropriate."

There went my relaxing afternoon.

Edna, the newer maid, opened the door to us, a worried look on her face.

"Mrs. Davis is just in here," she motioned toward the sitting room down the hall and, following us tentatively, announced us to the pathetic creature curled up in the crook of the sofa, asked if Christa needed anything else and scurried out.

"Oh, Miss Manley! How wonderful of you to come! My life has been ruined!" Christa threw her hand up to her head dramatically.

Miss Manley sat next to her and patted her hand while I looked around expecting to see, but hoping not to see, Monty Davis.

"He's gone! They've taken him away!"

"Who? Where?"

"Monty. They've taken him to prison."

"Surely not," Miss Manley said in her direct fashion. "If you are speaking of the police, then they have taken him in for questioning. Not prison."

"Oh," came the tiny voice.

"When did this happen, dear?" Miss Manley asked.

"Not too long ago. I've been frantic. I pleaded with them, I cried, I screamed. I'm afraid I acted very badly but Monty had nothing to do with that girl's death. He didn't even know her! He saw her perform twice and was interested in her purely as an artistic and economic matter to put her in some vehicle on Broadway."

I sat down in an adjacent chair, feeling awkward with her histrionics and what other revelations might be forthcoming.

"Dear girl," she said, addressing me, "would you ring for Edna?"

I obliged, finding the bell cord next to the mantel.

The timid maid came swiftly down the hall, yet entered the room gingerly, asking, "Ma'am?"

"Bring us the bottle and some ice."

Cocktails were evidently going to make things better. After some minutes in relative quiet except for Christa's sniffling and Miss Manley's hand patting, Edna returned and placed the alcohol, water, ice and glasses on the nearby table. A nod from Christa indicated the maid could leave and another nod in my direction was the signal to mix the drinks.

"No water for me," Christa said, so I poured her what must have been two shots' worth of gin with two hefty spoonsful of ice to dilute it. I didn't want to be responsible for her being drunk this early in the afternoon. She knocked down half of it in a gulp and exhaled loudly.

"Miss Manley, I have to confess, I have this horrible feeling that maybe Monty had met this girl before. I don't know why I think that." She gave a bit of a laugh. "Of course, I know why I think that. It's because he has flirted with young actresses before. Maybe more than flirted. I used to be one of those ingenues myself and you know how charming Monty can be."

I wouldn't have used that term but said nothing.

"These young girls throw themselves at the men in power and who can blame them? I may have done much the same myself at that age. I desperately wanted to be noticed, to succeed."

I wondered by her saying 'may have done' if she was not exactly admitting to the same behavior but also not ruling it out.

"I never met this Lulu Evans," Miss Manley said. "The only things I heard of her was that she was a magnetic performer and more than one young man was entranced by her."

"Who do you mean?" Christa sat up.

Realizing she had stepped into a trap of her own making, Miss Manley stammered a bit and then said, "Just some teenage boys who admired her from afar."

"You read about these things in the papers in New York, you know. Gangs of young men preying on women." Christa gulped the rest of her drink and sat forward on the sofa, holding up an accusing finger. "I'll bet that's what happened! You have to give the police their names. We can't let Monty suffer for the ill deeds of others."

Miss Manley became angry. "I'll do no such thing. There are no 'gangs' in Adams and certainly not containing anyone that I know. What possible motive could they have, to begin with?" She wasn't expecting an answer, but Christa jumped in anyway.

"Deviant behavior. All men are capable of it."

"Really!" Miss Manley scoffed. "The real question is: How did Lulu Evans come to be found on your doorstep of all the houses, woods and uninhabited places in the Berkshires?"

"Because we are so well known, of course. Jealousy. We've almost become immune to it but clearly someone had other ideas. Dear, pour me another." This last remark was directed at me, and hesitantly I obliged.

"Not so much ice," she added. "You have no idea what that dreadful Walter Winchell has said about us." She waited for a reaction from Miss Manley, who had no idea what she was talking about.

"The gossip columnist!" Christa said in a peeved tone. "Perhaps what he doesn't say but implies, dropping names together in a sentence and leaving it to the sordid imaginations of his readers to make the connection. We have been totally on the up and up in all our business dealings." She took several long sips of her drink and glared at us.

This conversation was going nowhere. "We're sorry to hear that, Miss Champion," I said. "We wish we could do something to help, but I'm afraid Miss Manley's niece is visiting, and we really should get back to her." I glanced over at one relieved face as I stood.

"Yes, Christa, we must be going," Miss Manley said, getting up quickly.

"Oh, nobody cares about me, anyway," she responded, managing to make her voice husky as if she were on the brink of tears.

I could see Miss Manley was about to start the sympathetic hand patting again in spite of herself, but I took her arm and thanked our hostess and propelled the both of us out of the room.

We hustled to the car before anyone came after us to implore us to stay and hear more of the sad tales of the famous couple or her strange ravings.

"Oh, dear," Miss Manley said as we sped away. "I probably should have had some of that gin, after all."

Chapter 14

John and I were at Dr. Mitchell's place the next morning preparing for a busy day when Inspector Gladstone unexpectedly showed up, looking grumpy and almost perplexed to see me there. I welcomed him politely, invited him to sit while I told the doctor of his arrival. I ushered the inspector into John's office and closed the door, then went to the kitchen to see if there was anything in the refrigerator but found it empty. What I did discover was that I could hear their conversation well through the wall and I couldn't keep myself from listening.

The inspector was annoyed at the entire Davis household—tenants and staff alike—for their seeming lack of observation skills. He claimed to be dumbfounded that nobody noticed the body on the doorstep until early in the morning and that Monty and Christa claimed not to recognize that it was Lulu Evans, whom they had just seen perform the night before, clad in the same outfit. It seemed that what Christa had thought was going to be a thorough grilling turned out to be disappointing from the police point of view.

"How is that possible?" He said raising his voice. "What the devil are these people playing at?"

John answered more softly that perhaps they were too rattled by the experience to think clearly.

Gladstone scoffed at the suggestion. "Your nurse was present, too, wasn't she? Let's get her in here for her recollection."

I moved quickly back through the hall, then turned just as the door to the consultation room opened, making it look as if I had just come from the reception area.

"Nurse Burnside, if you would...," John said to me, motioning me in and toward the empty chair facing his desk. I looked at him expectantly and he directed his gaze to the inspector.

"You accompanied Doctor Taylor up to Highfields Saturday morning, correct?"

"Yes."

"How would you describe the reactions of Mr. and Mrs. Davis?"

I looked at John, wondering where this line of questioning was going but he gave no indication.

"They seemed upset, of course. Christa was hysterical, I would say." I glanced back at John to see if I had overstepped my bounds by using the term hysterical, but he didn't react.

"Did they say they recognized the young woman or use her name?"

"Not that I recall, but we weren't the first ones there. Officer Reed had already gotten there."

"Don't you think it is odd that they saw her perform at the Mountain Aire the night before, yet didn't recognize her?"

"I didn't say they did or didn't recognize her, just that they didn't say anything in that vein when I was there. Also, I don't know at what point she was covered with a sheet and by whom."

Gladstone was quiet, looking down at the small notebook in his hands, yet he had written nothing down during our conversation.

"And she had the strange ability to look very different depending upon the circumstances."

"What do you mean by that?" His head jerked up.

"When I saw her earlier in the week about to rehearse with the band, she looked to be a fresh-faced teenager in casual clothes. When she performed, at least when I saw her twice, she had on evening clothes, her hair was pulled back and more formally styled, and she had theatrical makeup on. False eyelashes, I think, powder, rouge, lipstick."

John turned to me in slight surprise.

"Women notice these things," I said. "She was so...alive. And then to see her body so very still. And the blood on her head and face. The lack of animation made such a difference. And perhaps they didn't expect to find her on their doorstep."

"*If* they didn't have anything to do with her murder," Inspector Gladstone added as a qualifier. He paused. "Doctor Taylor, did you recognize her at once?"

"Yes, I saw her before her performance briefly when we were having dinner there a few days earlier, but my recollection is entirely of watching her sing twice. You're right," he said, looking at me. "She was such an animated individual in life that it took me a moment to realize who it was."

Inspector Gladstone got up slowly, not having heard anything to move his investigation forward. It seemed to me that there were so many people, mostly male, who took an interest in Lulu that could provide a motive to harm her. Rejected advances, jealousy about the interest of others, not to mention the heated rivalry that we witnessed between Cash Ridley and Monty Davis about who best could push her career forward. I wondered if anyone had related that conversation yet and decided that I would tell the Inspector when the time was right. My hesitation was not one of grandstanding but due to his disdain for me.

"Thank you," he said abruptly, shaking John's hand and nodding to me. They walked out the front door and, as I stood there, I noticed that John produced the folded paper from his pocket with the rose petals in it while explaining to the Inspector where he had found it and how it was identified. The Inspector nodded his head, looked back to me and glared as if I should have been the one to reveal this information to him, turned on his heel and went to his car.

John shrugged his shoulders at me as if to say that he had done a good deed that had gone unrewarded, and I shrugged in return.

***

Our usual lunch of sandwiches purchased in Adams at the café was consumed in John's dining room, a hasty meal because of the tight schedule that day. It was a far cry from the hot meal that Annie made, but it sufficed. We had just finished when the telephone in the office rang, and I heard Glenda's breathy voice.

"You'll never guess!"

"What?"

"Douglas Martin has been arrested!"

"What?" It seemed to be the only response I could muster.

"Yes! Inspector Gladstone and Officer Reed went to talk to him about an hour ago and he wasn't even up yet, if you can imagine. In his pajamas at the front door."

"How do you know that?"

"Annie, of course. Either looking out the window or hearing from Officer Reed. Anyway, they questioned him and allowed him to get dressed before they took him to the police station. And then the inspector and Officer Reed came back and went through the house."

"How do you know that?"

"By that time, Annie knew something was up, so I was at the windows. I saw them looking in his car, too, and putting things in an envelope. Oh, Aggie, you don't think I've been harboring a murderer, do you?"

"I couldn't say," I thought, remembering having seen in the back garden a blonde woman sitting on Douglas's lap who could have been Lulu. Was she just having fun, or was he considering her for a lead role in one of his plays? Or was she aware he was a playwright and angling for a stage career? In either case, I couldn't imagine that would constitute a motive for murder. If it was Lulu, that is.

"What am I going to do?" She wailed. "I won't have a tenant. There goes the rent!"

Now it seemed the rent was more of an issue than the possibility that Douglas Martin could be a murderer.

"We'll talk later," I said, hanging up.

I went back to the dining room and told John of the developments. He raised his eyebrows and sighed. "I'm afraid it was the petals that may have pointed the finger at him."

"How does that make any sense? What was she doing with Douglas Martin?" I stopped short, hoping I was mistaken and that it was someone else snuggling with him in his backyard.

John looked intently at me. "What do you know?"

I tried to qualify my response but the information I had was damning enough to implicate Glenda's tenant. "Maybe she was trying to ingratiate herself with him, knowing he was a playwright. Keeping her career options open." It sounded plausible. "If that was her."

"That doesn't explain why he would have killed her if he thought she was a promising actress."

"Unless she had a better offer from Monty Davis or from Cash Ridley. Both of those men seemed anxious to be responsible for her successful future career. You heard them squabbling over her in the ballroom."

"But Douglas Martin wasn't there to overhear it."

"True," I said. "But what if she had agreed to meet him after her performances and then, of course, the second one didn't happen because of the fire alarm. So, she met him and perhaps he reiterated his interest in her as his muse, or whatever, and she blurted that better offers were on the table?"

John gave me a strange look.

"It's a better explanation than roving gangs of young men preying on women."

"What are you talking about?"

"Christa Champion's idea of a motive. She was trying to protect her husband, who can obviously do that very well on his own. And I think she had too much to drink when she said it."

John shook his head as if to dispel the strange conversation we were having.

I kept thinking about Lulu Evans while I took the sterilized instruments out of the autoclave and all through the hour that I opened mail and wrote out the invoices from the end of last week's work. My mind started to wander toward Sophia, who had been absent in Hartford most of Friday although I didn't know when she and Bernard actually got back. Had she used the fire alarm and resultant chaos as an opportunity to confront her cousin about usurping her position with the Harry Williams Band? In turn, I began to wonder if Lulu had orchestrated her cousin's inflamed vocal cords but then remembered she hadn't taken over the vocalist position until Sophia became mute.

But was there a way of affecting someone's vocal cords without other physical damage to their mouth or throat? I asked John, who seemed surprised by my question and said he was not aware of any method of doing that.

"But, now that you mention it, I told Sophia that I would be looking in on her today as long as I was dropping in on Cash Ridley again. I am as concerned about his mental well-being as his physical health, based on what you told me about his behavior Sunday."

"That's kind of you."

"Why don't you come with me to the Mountain Aire? We'll close up shop now. I know, it's a bit early," he added as I glanced at my wristwatch. "You could do with an outing."

I thoroughly agreed although his smile was enough to have me say yes.

Chapter 15

It was another glorious summer day with flowers in full bloom along the sides of the road. The local gardens were bursting with the results of laborious tending in preparation for the Flower Show, which had been re-scheduled to mid-August due to an unexpected series of rainy days in July. The show was a hotbed of horticultural competition, more intense than the ongoing informal largest and sweetest tomato contest.

John had the hotel's front desk receptionist call Sophia's room to announce our arrival and we took the elevator, operated by the same elderly attendant, up to the fourth floor, which contained rooms for the staff who lived on site. Sophia opened the door to our knock and actually spoke, albeit in a whisper.

"How nice of you to come," she said, all smiles.

"Garbo Talks!" John replied, which got her laughing. He was referring to the latest advertising for the movie *Anna Christie* recently splashed in newspapers and magazines where Greta Garbo is first heard speaking.

"Don't I wish!" she said.

I noticed the stark difference in this room compared to Cash Ridley's suite, not just in size but in the style of furniture and the size of the window. There was only the one window, a single bed, dresser and two wooden chairs. Sophia looked momentarily embarrassed by the lack of another chair, not having expected to have two guests, but John relieved the tension by asking her to step over to the window for better light. I had brought the small flashlight from the office and shone it down her open throat while he positioned the mirrored instrument angled from the roof of her mouth.

"Much, much better. I don't know what magic the specialist did but it's quite an improvement." He withdrew the instrument, clearly happy with the results.

"He gave me a prescription and had me gargle with some powders, and it seems to have worked. Maybe it would have cleared up anyway and it was just a matter of time."

There was an awkward moment as we all stood until Sophia mentioned that she was expected downstairs to meet someone. I noticed a sign on the back of her door as we left, prohibiting smoking or guests in the room after five o'clock, and I guessed the lounge down the hall was an area with seating where the staff could interact. The tall bassist from the band was sitting reading a newspaper and smoking but got up as we approached to say hello to Sophia and introduce himself to us.

"Please, sit down. We didn't mean to disturb you," John said.

"Actually, Doc, I was hoping to ask you about something. Medical."

"Thank you again, Doctor," Sophia said, walking down the back stairs.

It was not unusual to be asked health questions and one doctor at the New York hospital where I trained said that, when people started that kind of a conversation in a social setting, he would jokingly ask them if they would like a full body exam right then and there. I smiled at the recollection but also thought that Lester looked like the kind of person who probably wouldn't mind pulling his shirt up to show the issue.

Before John could say anything, Lester held out his left hand and pointed to a lump between his index and middle finger.

"What do you make of that?" He was a large fellow and it looked strange for him to be fascinated by the small protrusion that he jiggled with his other hand.

"May I?" John asked, trying to inject some formality into the situation. After a nod from the musician, John reached out and manipulated the lump, which wobbled a bit under his touch.

"Does it hurt?"

"Nah. But I was worried about it and didn't want it to get in the way of my playing." He pushed it around. "Kind of a funny thing, huh?"

"What's that?" John asked, turning Lester's right hand over that had white powder under the fingernails.

Lester laughed. "Not what you think. It's rosin for my bass bow. I usually keep it in my case, which has gone missing. Not that I use rosin or the bow that much. I do the plucking more for rhythm."

John looked back at the lump curiously and then resumed. "I can't be sure, but it seems that you have some sort of a cyst."

Lester's curious expression turned to one of concern. "What does that mean?"

"Nothing much, really. It's just a little lump of something that decided to grow there. It could just as easily disappear. It probably won't get any larger but if it does and gets in the way of your music making, it can be easily removed."

Lester smiled. "Funny that this should be on my fingering hand." He shrugged.

"If it does change in any way, call the office and we'll take a look."

"Thanks, Doc. What do I owe you?"

John looked at me and smiled with an idea. "How about the next time I am in the ballroom, you dedicate a song to me?"

Lester held up a finger. "No, better yet. How about if I dedicate a solo?"

"That works for me!" They shook hands and laughed.

"I've got to see someone else," John said, excusing himself and starting to go toward the elevator.

"There are back stairs, you know," Lester said. "It's what *we're* supposed to use. He flicked his finger under his large nose to indicate what he thought of the different treatment of guests and staff down to which staircase they used.

We went down the uncarpeted flight that was wide enough to accommodate people carrying towels or sheets as far down as the basement laundry, but we pushed the door open at the third floor where the Ridley suites were located.

"What did he mean about the powder on his hand?" I asked.

"You know how people think musicians are always hopped up on something. Cocaine."

I was startled enough by his comment to not respond.

"If your experience with musical people is family playing the piano in the evening after dinner, I'm not surprised that you didn't pick up on his reference." Looking around he continued, "Here we are among the paying guests, I suppose," referring to the carpeting and wide windows at either end of the hall, brightening the area considerably more than the fourth floor.

Bernard let us into the business suite where Cash was sitting on the couch, reading through some papers and Catherine was at one of the desks typing at an impressive speed. She did not stop when we entered and Cash stood to greet us, merely speaking more loudly to be heard above the racket.

"Why don't we go into my personal suite?" He led the way into the adjoining rooms that were as large as the ones we had come from except there was a bedroom through a set of double doors off to the side. I nodded to John and stepped back into the business suite to allow the exam to be done in private and sat on the now-unoccupied sofa. Catherine stopped her typing.

"How nice to see you again," she said.

"Same here. Please, I didn't mean to interrupt your work."

She scoffed, got up and came to sit by me while Bernard put away the papers that Cash had left behind. "I need to take a break now and then. Besides, I wanted to set up a tennis date."

"If your backhand is as fast as your typing, you've got me scared!"

Bernard laughed and said, "It is. Watch out!"

"Good, I usually play with some very timid girls who volley the ball right back at my racquet, which makes for an easy win but no fun."

"You'll get a run for your money from me. Nobody calls me timid on a tennis court!"

"What's the news in West Adams?" Bernard asked, sorting the papers into order.

I assumed he was talking about the investigation into Lulu's death, not the prediction on who would win the Best Dahlia prize at the Flower Show. "They've arrested someone."

"Who?"

"Oddly enough, he rents the house next door to where I am staying. I've met him once and he seemed harmless enough." That wasn't an apt description of my impression of him, but it would do.

"It's the harmless-looking guys who end up being the most vicious," Catherine said with enough venom that she had to be speaking from experience.

"Did he know her well?" Bernard looked at Catherine. "I wonder if he ever came up here to watch her perform?" She shrugged her shoulders.

"I don't know what motive they think he had," I said, although I had my suspicions, not that I was going to share them or reveal what evidence linked him to Lulu. It would come out in good time.

Catherine gave a shiver as if to ward off further thoughts of what had happened to the young woman and changed the subject. "Do you have time tomorrow for a set?"

"If it's toward the end of the day, say five or six o'clock?" I replied.

"Hah! She wants to get you with the sun in your eyes," Bernard teased, moving toward his desk. He busied himself with filing papers and writing while Catherine and I talked about Sophia, and I reported that she seemed to be doing much better and was in better spirits.

"What a horrible thing to have happened."

The door to the bedroom suite opened and John came out to the expectant looks of Cash's employees.

"All is well," he said in that vague way that meant 'not to worry but I can't give you details.' It seemed to calm whatever concerns they had, and we said goodbye, hearing the clacking of the typewriter keys as we left.

"Is he all right?" I asked.

"I think so. He should stop smoking, lose weight, get exercise and be in a less stressful business. Not only intuitive advice, but suggestions he has undoubtedly heard before. We can only do so much with noncompliant patients."

We took the elevator to the lobby and, hearing some music emanating from the ballroom, walked over to sneak a peek at the rehearsal in progress. We slipped into the room and sat at the rear while the band was reaching a crescendo and Harry Williams, shirtsleeves rolled up, banged his baton on the music stand, breaking the stick in pieces that skittered across the floor.

"What the hell are you guys doing? Taking a nap? Wake up— you sound awful. Jeez!"

He began again and stopped them a short while into the phrase. "Gene," he said, addressing the saxophonist. "Give it a little gas, huh?" He mocked the discomfort on the other man's face, but Gene responded by blowing a raspberry with his instrument.

"You clown!" Harry said, raising what remained of his baton and was about to throw it before his eye caught the motion of Sophia coming into the room and then saw us as well. It made him stop short.

"Well, hello folks," he said, suddenly all smiles. "Come to hear how magic is made?"

Gene obliged by blowing as hard as he could, and it got the bandmates sniggering.

"Take five," Harry scowled and waved them away. "Sophia, my dear. How are you doing?"

"Much better, thank you." It was still the whispery tone.

"Doesn't sound like you'll be warbling anytime soon," he said.

"I've been advised to continue to rest my voice."

Harry puffed out his cheek and blew out the air in frustration. "Doc, what do you think?"

John was surprised to be asked to comment on a patient's condition to someone else, but Sophia nodded, silently giving her permission.

"I think she's doing exactly what the specialist advised her to do. You can't rush these things."

Harry put his hands on his hips and shook his head. "This place is going to kill me. First, I think we've signed up for some Podunk joint and it turns out to be swell, then I got Sophia here to sign on, which was great, and then she loses her voice and who comes to the rescue but Lulu.

What a voice, what a delivery, the audience eating out of her hand. Damn girl." He turned and made his way back to the empty bandstand, pulled a cigarette out of his pocket and lit it with a gold lighter. It was a good thing he wasn't looking in our direction anymore to see the hurt and fury in Sophia's face at his crass, cruel statement.

Chapter 16

I found Glenda drinking coffee in the kitchen with Annie, who told me that Officer Reed had just left. I sat knowing that there was likely some good information about Lulu Evans' death but waited for one of them to bring it up, and sure enough, Glenda could not keep it to herself.

"Officer Reed interviewed the band members yesterday in their rooms and he was properly shocked by what he said was their language and untidy habits. He said that Gladstone told him musicians of their type often indulged in drugs."

"Did he see any of that behavior?"

"No…but I think that is a common concept of what they do."

"I was just there and didn't notice anything strange." Except the bassist's comment about powder on his hand. "It's an odd place. They have small rooms compared to the rest of the hotel but a communal lounge area to make up for it. But I guess that's what they provide to the help."

"I bet Mrs. Lewis is glad that Roger is not living on the grounds. They could be a terrible influence on a young man," Annie said. She got up to put her cup and saucer in the sink before taking some items out of the pantry in preparation for supper.

"But the most amazing thing is that Douglas Martin, taken all the way to Pittsfield to be questioned, has been released from custody. My tenant is free, and I'll get my rent."

That was surprising, and I waited for her to elaborate.

"It seems his girlfriend, someone from the City, was with him on Friday night. Going to spend the weekend with him." Glenda raised her eyebrows. "They went out to visit friends somewhere or other and didn't get back until very late or early, depending upon how you look at it. Officer Reed says he was a bit vague about the time except that it was dark but concluded that alcohol consumption may have impaired his memory. Anyway, they came back home and found Lulu Evans. Dead. On the doorstep! My doorstep!"

"The petals," I said.

"Yes, that must be where they came from. And now the preposterous part of the story. He claims he was so unnerved by finding a deceased young woman there with his girlfriend Lois something-or-other furious at him thinking he had been two-timing her. But he said he didn't recognize the girl and had no idea who she was. So, instead of doing the sensible thing, calling the police, which he didn't because he thought Officer Reed didn't like him, he persuaded his girlfriend to help him load Lulu into the trunk of his car to move the body elsewhere."

"Can you imagine?" Annie asked in an outraged tone.

"What was he thinking?" It was all I could manage to say.

"Not much, evidently. Of all the things, he decides to dump her on Montgomery Davis's doorstep, whether it was the first remote place he could think of or for revenge about the producer's treatment of him."

I think my mouth was wide open at the point. "That *is* an incredible story."

"He is sticking to it."

Annie tut-tutted and shook her head at the perfidy of men.

"So, the police are back at the beginning, not knowing who did it." Glenda said.

"If Douglas is telling the truth," Annie muttered.

Glenda didn't like that comment at all.

"It could be anybody. It could have been Monty Davis," I said.

"That's right! You said he had seen Lulu and made comments about wanting her to be in one of his productions. Maybe he approached her and she refused, and he became angry."

"And what? Because he thought so little of Douglas's writing he decided to dump her in front of his door?"

"But did Mr. Davis know where Douglas lived?" Annie asked.

"He must have seen the address on the script that was sent to him," Glenda said.

"Where was Christa all this time?"

"She was his accomplice!" Glenda said, holding her index finger up for emphasis.

We were quiet a moment, but I had to say, "That seems like a far-fetched explanation. Would you help Stuart cover up a murder?"

"Of course not!" Glenda responded. "What if Christa was jealous of Lulu and she killed her? And then Monty helped her put the body next door?"

"Christa Champion? You've seen her. She might be ninety pounds soaking wet and Lulu was a strong and healthy girl."

"The blunt instrument. Or Mickey Finn," Glenda said, her eyes widening.

"Who in the world is that?" Annie asked, turning from her potato peeling,

"Not who, but what. It means somebody could have slipped something into her drink to make her unconscious. And then hit her with something."

All three of us stopped talking. It was an interesting theory, but I knew of someone who had just such drugs at his disposal.

Chapter 17

The next day seemed to be one for tonsillitis at the doctor's office, with two mothers bringing in two children each to be checked out. How miserable for them to be on summer vacation from school and have to stay home sick. I felt bad for the families and also realized the mothers would have the lion's share of the burden of taking care of them, bringing up trays and thinking of ways to distract them until they were well enough to resume outdoor activities.

I assisted the doctor by setting up the examination room and asking the older of Mrs. Connelly's boys to get up on the table, figuring he would need to set the bar for bravery. He looked particularly despondent and, when asked by the doctor if his throat hurt, managed to say no although looking over the doctor's shoulders during the exam, I could see his tonsils were red and swollen.

"Will I have to have them out?" he asked, looking scared for the first time.

Doctor Taylor addressed him directly. "I don't think so just yet. Let's try something for a few days and see if things calm down. I'll write you a prescription."

"Shouldn't he have them out, though?" the mother asked.

"Although I can do the surgery, it is best done in Pittsfield's hospital, with a two-day stay, which might be expensive. If little brother here needs to have it done as well, it would then be twice the cost, of course."

Mrs. Connelly's mouth twisted at this information, and she nodded her head in comprehension. Her other child was examined with the same results and advice.

"I heard you get to eat ice cream when you get your tonsils out," the smaller boy said.

"Yes, you do. But perhaps if you're good, you'll get ice cream anyway."

The second mother, who overheard some of the conversation when the examination door was opened to release the two boys pushing past each other, hoped her son and daughter would be given the same prescription, and they were. I was surprised, knowing the New York hospital where I trained was moving away from routine tonsillectomies in favor of being more cautious; however, I imagined a rural practitioner might be following older recommendations from medical school when parents and doctors favored surgery rather than leaving the tonsils in.

Something about my reaction or manner must have alerted John because he smiled at me after both families had left.

"Surprised?" he asked.

"Yes, I am. They were certainly quick to take mine out back when."

"Poor thing," he said patting my shoulder and smiling. "I do read the medical journals, you know, and the pendulum has been swinging in the other direction for a while."

The touch sent a distinct and pleasant shiver down my arm. He did have a lovely smile. When he turned away, I blinked to shrug the sensations away and resumed my seat at the desk in the waiting room.

One more mother with a sore-throated child showed up before the end of the day and was given the same prescription and advice. Aside from the three visits, it had been a quiet afternoon with no phone calls. At five, I put my head into the open door of John's office and let him know I was leaving for the afternoon. That smile again.

***

Glenda let me borrow her car to drive over to the Mountain Aire for my tennis game with Catherine while the sun was still high enough in the sky. I was feeling happy sitting in what I pretended to be my car, enjoying my job and increasingly comfortable and confident in my abilities. And here I was, young woman of the world, taking on a game of tennis with an assistant to a high-profile executive, just like any other professional woman. I was no longer so interested in the gossipy tea gatherings of Miss Manley's although on one level they were a bit of a guilty pleasure, and it was amazing to acknowledge the information network that the women in West Adams had developed. But I was intrigued by Catherine Hastings and what seemed to be her independent lifestyle in the City and getting to accompany her boss on a long working vacation.

Catherine was a bit flushed as she greeted me in the lobby, and I hoped it wasn't because she had warmed up ahead of me as we chatted our way out to the courts. Who should be there but Roger, surprised to see me in other than a nurse's uniform or casual clothes, and he stared a little too long at my mostly bare legs.

"Hello," I said. "I hear you have racquets on loan for those of us who forgot to pack them."

"Sure thing, Miss Burnside." He trotted off to a nearby shed and retrieved several for me to choose from.

"It seems this job suits you," I commented, turning one over to get a better feel for the handling. He certainly seemed more self-assured, tan from hours in the sun and I noticed he now sported sunglasses. He was bound to wow the girls at school in September. I chose the lighter- weight racquet with the longest handle and bounced a ball several times to get the familiar feel, remembering the pleasure of whacking a ball against a backboard toward the end of my day at the summer camp, a mindless yet satisfying activity like swimming laps.

"Uh-oh," said Catherine, tucking the crucifix into the top of her blouse. "I think I ought to be very afraid."

I laughed at her. "I don't think so. It's been a while since I've played, and I can tell you're going to have a wicked serve."

She smiled and walked to her end of the court, her tan right arm offset by a thin gold chain as she bounced the ball against the clay. "Ready?"

I could feel Roger's eyes on us, which made me even more eager to show off what skills I had left. Even though I positioned myself well back on the court, her serve whizzed by, landing inches in front of the end line and crashing into the chain link fence behind.

"Fifteen-love," she called out.

This was going to be a short and painful set.

Catherine was incredibly good and with each stroke I noticed how strong she was, but she hadn't counted on my long reach, and I was able to volley it back more than I thought possible. The second set was over, and she called out to me to take a break. We sat on a sideline bench, wiping the sweat from our foreheads with towels provided by Roger, and gulped down the glasses of water he brought us.

I laughed as I caught my breath. "Catherine, I have a feeling you've been playing tennis quite a while."

"Just one of those local teenage champs in Connecticut. Some folks wanted me to go into it professionally, but my parents were against it, with good reason."

"What were their reservations?"

"It was all right to be the country club star and play on the high school team. They didn't think it was a respectable thing to do for a living and neither did I."

I still didn't get it and looked at her quizzically.

"You know. The kind of women who engage in sports for a living, such as it is."

"Oh," was all that I could manage, not sure what kind of women those were. Rough? Uncouth? Not country club types? Or did she mean manly women? I decided not to pursue it.

"Anyway, I wanted to be a career woman. I went to junior college and then Katie Gibbs, *Katherine Gibbs*, if you please." She winked at me. "It was a lot more work than I imagined but I got more out of it than the previous two years of Fine Arts classes and French in college. The cachet of Gibbs got me good job right after graduation and two years after that, CR poached me from my former employer." She was all smiles, and I could understand her pride at having someone of Cash Ridley's stature seeking her out. "I've had a good career so far."

Of course, I wondered about her romantic life—her relationship with CR seemed entirely professional as was that with Bernard. Maybe not. They were in close contact every day and he was a good-looking and charming man from what I knew of him. He seemed to be CR's right-hand man and if his story about his ex-wife was correct, was possibly in line to inherit the business or at least part of the Ridley fortune.

We finished our water and Roger took the pitcher and glasses away while we switched court sides.

"If you don't mind me saying so, Aggie, you would do better not to be so polite in your game."

I couldn't imagine what she was referring to.

"Women have a tendency to volley to the opponent, which makes for a pleasant pastime but will hardly put you in the winner's circle. Hit the ball to the place where I am not, if you want to win. Study your opponent—is her backhand weak? Does she like to hang back in a certain spot? Make her run to return the ball."

I had learned tennis at an all-girls' camp where, of course, the point was to volley until someone made a mistake. That was how you won, not by deliberately making your opponent falter. I had fallen into my old habits.

"Of course! Well, look out!" I served with energy and with her advice in my head made sure to get her running back and forth across the court as she had done to me. Two points later and we were laughing at our achievement.

I heard a commotion that sounded like Roger yelling, "Hey!" and I thought he was being cheeky at our spirited game. But he continued shouting as he approached, and we stopped to see what the matter was.

"Is Doc Taylor here?" he said, his face red from running.

"No, I came by myself. Whatever is the matter?" Of course, I immediately thought that CR was having some medical issue.

"Come quickly," he said, and turned to run back into the hotel. Both of us followed him at a trot and caught up at the elevator, where he ushered us in, panting heavily. He looked disturbed enough that I didn't dare ask what the problem was.

We stopped at the fourth floor, and he ran out toward the back stairs, pointing to where a group of staff and musicians stood, obscuring the view of what was of interest. They parted as we came close, and it took a moment to make sense of what I was seeing. It was a maid in her uniform, stuffed awkwardly into a laundry trolley, her head at a strange angle and a towel partly obscuring her face.

I laid my hand on her arm and felt it was still warm but putting my index and middle finger on her carotid artery where a necklace was twisted, I felt no pulse whatsoever. She was dead.

Chapter 18

Catherine peered over my shoulder and gripped my arm, her nails digging into the skin.

"It's Constance!"

I just stared at her, surprised she knew the staff member's name.

"Bernard's wife. His ex-wife," she explained.

I swung my head around to look more closely and saw the initials CS on a heart on the necklace. We heard the rumble of footsteps coming down the hall to investigate and as many maids, workers and staff as the hotel had begun to fill the corridor.

"It's getting stuffy in here," Catherine said in a small voice, her face pale and her breathing shallow.

"Let her sit down," I said, pushing my way through the group to a chair by the wall. I sat her down, put her head between her knees and commanded her to breath slowly and deeply, in and out.

It was an awful scene with each person feeling compelled to rush up to the laundry bin, look inside and gasp, some of the women pointing decisively at the body and claiming it was Carol. Perhaps Catherine had made a mistake—why would Bernard's ex-wife be working at the Mountain Aire?

We found out some time later when he came slowly up the hall, perhaps warned by others of the impending sight, put two hands on the side of the bin, leaned over and groaned. He put his hands to his face and sobbed. Now CR was striding down the hall and, seeing Bernard crumpled over in grief, ran the remaining steps, looked in the basket and said nothing. He simply turned away with eyes closed. I asked CR and Bernard to sit down, fearing a collapse and they did so, only Bernard weeping.

It was a chaotic scene as the Fosters, father and son, showed up and assessed the situation immediately, taking the initiative to ask people to step away or get back to work. It was still some time before Inspector Gladstone from Pittsfield arrived with an officer in tow. His very presence made the remaining onlookers back away, some drifting off entirely before his gaze fell on me with a look of initial surprise and then suspicion.

I felt I had to explain my presence and did so, which didn't mollify him. He stepped forward and looked into the bin, reached down to ascertain that she was dead and began the usual questions of who discovered the body and what time that was. From the back of the lingering crowd came the band's drummer, raising his hand slightly to acknowledge he was the one.

To my surprise, he began questioning the man, whose name turned out to be Albert, right there in front of the family. I started to say something, but a glare from the inspector made me go quiet. As much as I thought it inappropriate, it wasn't my place.

Albert told the inspector that the band had rehearsed new numbers much of the day, taking a break at lunch and another one before the end of the day when they would change for the evening's performance. He had come up to his room, got his Dopp bag and was heading for the shared men's bathroom to wash and shave when he noticed the laundry bin along the wall partly in his path. As he went to move it, he noticed it was unusually heavy, looked in and saw the body of Carol, the maid.

"Constance," CR corrected him in a wooden tone.

"Which is it?" Gladstone asked, looking around.

"It's my daughter. Constance," CR said.

The woman who had previously said the maid was Carol stepped forward with a determined look on her face.

"No, it's Carol. She just started a week ago. Her room's down there."

We exchanged looks all around.

"Well, which is it?"

Bernard stopped his crying, took out a handkerchief, blew his nose, wiped his eyes and stood up. "It's my wife, Constance. I thought I saw her over the weekend out on the terrace, but it seemed impossible. I hung back after the others finished their lunch and I saw it was her. She was here. Living here just one floor above. And I didn't know."

Gladstone had pushed his hat back on his head and screwed up his eyes in disbelief.

"Oh, really?" He turned to the officer who had come with him, whispered instructions and whirled back in our direction. The officer discreetly went toward the elevator.

"She said she wanted to tell me something important, but it wasn't the right time," Bernard added. "I guess I'll never know what it was."

Inspector Gladstone said, "As soon as Officer Mallory finishes his phone calls, all of you are coming downstairs and we are going to sort this out."

"You can use one of the smaller salon rooms on the first floor," Foster said and stepped back.

More footsteps were heard coming up the back stairs and Harry Williams, wide-eyed and out of breath, came into view.

"What's going on?" He looked at each of us and then at Gladstone.

I let the inspector give the minimal details he chose to share, and Harry stood stock still with his mouth hanging open.

"Where are the rest of the guys?"

Albert shrugged. "Maybe downstairs having a smoke. I was the first one to come back up. Beard, you know," he said, running his hand against the rasping dark cheek and chin of someone who might have to shave twice a day.

Those of us who were standing looked for a place to sit while we waited for the return of the officer who probably made a call for an ambulance. Once he had come back and nodded to the inspector, we pulled ourselves together and made our way down to the first floor, following the Fosters' lead.

"Let's put everyone in one room while I take folks one by one in another one," Gladstone said. He poked his head around the corner of one of the side rooms off the ballroom and said, "This'll do fine." He motioned with his head for Albert, the person who had found the body, to go in ahead and the door closed behind them.

George Foster, Senior, led us into an adjacent room. We sat in the chairs that encircled a round table covered with a tablecloth and he then left. I was appalled by the inspector's lack of respect or sympathy, no matter who the woman was, and his crude way of making it seem like we were all somehow suspects.

Foster came back a few minutes later, followed by a waiter who brought a carafe of coffee, a pitcher of water, cups and glasses. The maid Muriel introduced herself and Catherine and I shared our names, but Bernard and CR were silent. Both of them looked haggard. Muriel glanced at me expectantly and I assumed she thought I ought to be the one to pour coffee. I obliged and we handed the filled cups around the table, then the cream and sugar. It was something to do.

I looked over at Muriel, who was sipping her black coffee delicately, glancing from under her lashes as if anxious about making an etiquette mistake. She was probably in her mid-thirties, but I had noticed from my hospital training that hard work aged people prematurely and she might have been closer to my age. I gave her a small smile. She may have thought I was looking at her roughened fingers, and she put the coffee cup down quickly and placed her hands in the lap of her uniform.

We sat in silence for some minutes before CR shouted, "What in hell was she doing here?" We flinched as he turned toward Bernard and I thought he might punch him in the face.

"I don't know," Bernard said in a calm voice. "Perhaps she hoped to make amends with you."

"With me? You were the one who divorced her! I had my own reasons to disown her."

Bernard fidgeted with the coffee spoon.

"Despite what we told you, we never signed the divorce papers. We both hoped to reconcile somehow." His baleful look at CR was pathetic. So, he didn't want to publicly mend the marriage because of his father-in-law? That didn't make sense. None of this made sense.

Inspector Gladstone appeared in the doorway and beckoned to Muriel, who looked from side to side as if to ascertain to whom he was motioning. I thought it incredibly rude of him, a demeaning way to treat the poor woman who had no more involvement in this business except having worked with the dead woman.

They were gone in conversation—or interrogation, probably—for only fifteen minutes, which had to exhaust what little she may have known of the woman she called Carol. She did not return to our waiting room although Gladstone came back to the doorway. I imagined he was going to beckon to me, so I decided not to look in his direction or make eye contact. If he wished to speak to me, he'd better well come into the room and ask. I could hear a huffing noise, which was probably his annoyance, but I was not giving in and demurely sipped my coffee while the others turned in his direction.

"Miss Burnside," he said, suddenly at my shoulder. In a voice dripping with sarcasm and a phony accent he added, "would you be so kind as to accompany me to the salon?"

I nodded politely, seeing the others around the table notice the friction, and walked out, head held high. I knew he was dying to know what I was doing at the scene of a murder. Again. But I wasn't going to be intimidated by his bad disposition and predilection to assume everyone had something to hide. We walked into the adjacent room, and I sat down with dignity in the chair opposite his seat, where his notebook was open to view. There wasn't much written in it from his previous interview: Muriel's full name, an address, a number that could have been years working at the hotel, the name Carol underlined several times and some jottings that I could not read before having to sit down.

He glared at me, seeing that I had glanced at the notebook.

"Amateur detective, are we?" he sneered.

"Certainly not. What do you mean?"

"What were you doing orchestrating the murder scene when I arrived?"

Now I was getting annoyed with his assumption. "I was doing nothing of the sort. I had been playing tennis with Catherine Hastings when Roger came running out to the courts, asking if the

130

doctor were here. He wasn't, so Roger asked me to come upstairs because something had happened."

"Why did he call you?"

"He knows that I am a nurse and I suppose he thought I could help."

"What did you think had happened?"

"My first thought was that one of the guests may have had a medical emergency."

Gladstone had what I would call beady eyes, dark and menacing. He was trying to use them to full effect in intimidating me.

"And?"

"He brought us—Catherine came with me, perhaps thinking Mr. Ridley had some emergency—up to the fourth floor."

"Why did you think Mr. Ridley had a medical problem?"

I considered a moment and thought it safe to say, "Because he had some incidents in the past and she was concerned about her employer, I presume. The elevator attendant was not on duty for some reason and once we saw that Roger pressed the button for the fourth floor without speaking, she and I assumed that it involved someone else. Perhaps one of the musicians who were staying on that floor during their engagement here at the hotel."

"How do you know that?"

"The doctor and I visited another resident of that floor just yesterday. Sophia Evans, if you must know."

"Evans?" he asked looking up.

"She had seen the doctor and he was following up with her. As we left, we encountered one of the band members and that's how I surmised the fourth floor housed the staff, so to speak. Or perhaps the staff who did not live locally. I'm sure Mr. Foster can fill you in on those details." I realized I sounded snooty, but I didn't care. There was something repellent about his method of interrogation.

"I'll be sure to do that, *Nurse* Burnside. Is there anything else you know that you would like to tell me? Or not tell me but should."

I held my temper in check and paused as if to wrack my brains for any other information.

"No, I think that is all I know." I managed a tight smile.

He stood and I was more than happy to leave but went into the other room to briefly let Catherine know that I was going back to West Adams. The three of them who were left—CR, Bernard and Catherine—were seated where I had left them, looking anxious.

How could I not be consumed with questions as I drove home? Bernard revealed he wasn't divorced and seemed devastated by her death, but when he told me about her the previous week as we were dancing, he sounded cavalier about it. Saying she was hardly constant. Was he now regretting his treatment of her? What was she doing there, anyway? Of course, there was the chance that CR—her own father—might recognize her, too. Perhaps Catherine, too, although I didn't know if they knew one another. What was the thing that Constance was going to tell Bernard? It must have been explosive information if she had to be so secretive about it. And then to be killed before telling anyone. I wondered if perhaps she had written something down and left it in her room at the hotel. But I wasn't going to be the one to look for it.

That was Inspector Gladstone's job.

I had barely pulled into the driveway when Glenda came rushing out to meet me.

"Roger called home and told Nina and the reverend what had happened at the Mountain Aire!"

As she walked me into the house, she said word had passed through the town although very few people knew who CR was, much less the situation concerning his daughter. But still, it was sensational gossip for this sleepy neck of the woods. Before I had entered the house, Glenda told me someone from the Pittsfield Police Department called Officer Reed, who in turn had reported to Annie, over a cup of coffee and a slice of pound cake, that Bernard had been arrested and they were transporting him to Pittsfield. That was quick! It seemed obvious to Gladstone that the murder was about an inheritance, although that didn't make sense if CR had already cut his daughter off financially. What would Bernard have to gain by her death? He must have retained some affection for her if they had not followed through with the divorce and he seemed genuinely upset by the event.

"I really need to sit down," I said, entering the sitting room as Glenda hovered nearby waiting for details from me.

Miss Manley had heard the car pull in and was alert to my agitated state of mind.

"Glenda, dear, why don't you get some tea for us?" she asked.

"Thank you," I said to Miss Manley. I breathed in and out slowly, composing my mind to think of nothing and watching her knitting needles as they clicked along at a pleasing rhythm. I was grateful that she didn't press me for information. My luck did not hold as Glenda came back into the room too soon.

"Annie's taking care of it," she told Miss Manley and plopped down on the sofa next to me, her hands covering her growing stomach. She let a few seconds go by before saying, "Well?"

"Well, what? You seem to know all there is to know already." I sounded peeved, and I was, but I relented and told them both what I had witnessed as Glenda's eyes grew wide and Miss Manley kept up the pace of knitting.

"And now you know more than I do, having heard what Officer Reed was told."

"What a terrible burden for Mr. Ridley," Miss Manley said.

"Oddly enough, he seemed more angry than anything," I said.

"I understood that he and his daughter were estranged," Glenda added.

"But you know that makes it so much harder, my dear," Miss Manley said, shaking her head.

Chapter 19

The tea group was at Miss Manley's the next day and despite the number of women who attended, only two of them were perennial hostesses. I came to learn later that they volunteered for the duty because of the size of their sitting rooms, the presence of a maid or cook to assist with the refreshments, and the lack of children or other family members getting in the way or overhearing the often-candid comments of the participants.

As usual, I came in midway through the function straight from work and didn't dare go upstairs to change for fear of missing out on some tidbit. Glenda had saved me a seat and by the look in her eye I knew a juicy topic was being discussed.

"Bernard," she whispered.

"I can't believe the police in Pittsfield would do such a thing. Aren't they concerned for the welfare of women in this community?" Mrs. Proctor asked.

Glenda whispered, "They let him go."

I took a sugar cookie from the plate on the table.

Miss Olsen was similarly affronted. "From what I hear, this is the second murder he committed in a short period of time. Both women. And one of them his wife!"

The murmurings sounded like angry bees, and I noticed Miss Tierney looked over at me for confirmation.

"You were there, weren't you?"

The room became instantly silent. I swallowed my mouthful and nodded my head. Clearly, they were expecting more from me than that.

"I didn't discover the body. I came on the scene when Roger came out to the tennis courts looking for the doctor and had me go into the building as the most available medical person, I suppose."

"How horrible."

"Yes, it was terrible. Poor woman," I added.

Nina spoke up. "Actually, Roger told me that the reason Bernard was released was that he had been with his employer, Mr. Ridley, the entire afternoon."

Heads swiveled in her direction.

"Of course, he might say that," Miss Ballantine said. Why she was so certain, I could not be sure.

"Was he with his employer *every minute* of the afternoon? Did no one take a break, use the restroom, for example?"

One of the women tittered.

"That's possible, I suppose," I said. But he was on the third floor and the woman—his wife—was one floor above. Surely he would have been seen if he had used the elevator because there is usually an attendant on duty." I stopped myself and remembered that the attendant wasn't there when Roger took Catherine and me upstairs. "Besides, the fourth floor has so many residents and activity, I can't imagine he wouldn't have been seen." I then also remembered that Albert said he was the only one there when he went to the men's room to shave. Could Bernard have sneaked up while no one was about? Or could Albert have killed her? But, why?

It might have been my perplexed expression that made the conversation die down briefly before the topic of Mona Strathern came up again, another safe subject since her mother was not present.

"You'll be pleased to know that Mona, whom many of you were worried about, is not only safe at home, but has given up illusions of running away to New York City," Miss Manley said.

"Is she locked in her room?" Mrs. Rockmore asked, not intending to be funny, but it got a good round of laughter.

"I understand that she came to her senses when she realized Douglas Martin has had for some time a steady girlfriend whom he liked to keep under wraps," Glenda said. "I'll bet he thought I might charge him more rent if I knew."

"You mean they are living together?" someone asked.

Oh dear, Glenda had stepped in it this time, I thought.

A quick recovery was in order as she didn't want anyone to think she condoned what was called 'shacking up.'

"No, no. She comes up to visit from time to time. Everything on the up and up. There are three bedrooms in my house, you know." As if they would be sleeping separately.

It was a weak defense, and everyone knew it, but no one wanted to pursue it. It was getting time for everyone to go home and start dinner and it was generally felt that these gatherings should end on a positive note.

"Well, dear," Miss Ballantine said, addressing the hostess, "thank you for a lovely tea. Let's hope that Eleanor Strathern will be able to join us next week."

The women stood, brushed off their skirts and left the tea things on the end tables and coffee table knowing that Glenda and I would help Miss Manley clean up. This seemed to have been the tradition ever since we younger women took part, and we didn't mind since we could eat the leftover refreshments.

I got a large tray from the kitchen and, pausing, saw that Annie had left a folded note for Miss Manley. Bringing it back to the sitting room, I gave it to her as Glenda and I stacked the saucers and cups.

"Oh, dear," Miss Manley said, twisting her mouth to the side. "Christa again. She wants to talk to me." She sighed.

"Perhaps it's nothing to worry about," Glenda said.

The look Miss Manley gave her said it all: there was always drama where Christa was concerned.

"I'll call her. I hope she doesn't want to come here. She may stay longer than I'd like, and I don't want to feel trapped."

She left to call from the telephone in the kitchen and returned shortly to report that she had best go up to Highfields because Christa was slurring her words, Monty wasn't there, and Miss Manley certainly didn't want her driving in her condition.

"Would you mind driving me, Aggie?" she asked, and I could tell Glenda was a bit put out that she wouldn't get to see the drama.

Alice answered the door, a furrow of concern on her forehead.

"Thank goodness. Mr. Davis left in a temper some time ago and I'm afraid Mrs. Davis is not doing too well." Her meaning was clear.

"Oh, Miss Manley!" came the impassioned voice from the sitting room. I could almost imagine that she had put her hand to her forehead in distress like the actresses in a silent movie melodrama.

We were barely into the room when she exploded, "You cannot believe the agony I have been in these past days." She looked in our direction and didn't seem to mind my being there, then waved toward the armchairs for us to be seated since she was sprawled on the sofa.

"May I get you ladies something to drink?" Alice asked, nodding toward the highball glass on the coffee table in front of Christa, the liquid nearly down to the bottom.

"Just water, thank you," I said, answering for us both.

"How have you been?" Miss Manley said, a very normal way to begin a conversation that seemed funny under the circumstances.

"Not well. Not well at all."

There was an awkward pause. Alice took the hint and left the room. Christa looked at Miss Manley, seated with her back straight, her hat and gloves still on, clutching her handbag, then at me, and made a decision.

"I have something shocking and important to tell Miss Manley and I need you to swear not to tell a soul."

"Of course," I said.

"I mean it. You cannot tell anyone." She was slurring her words again and I hoped she was not going to down the remainder of her drink.

"Nurse Burnside is a professional, Christa. She certainly knows how to keep a confidence."

"You promise you won't think less of me?" she said looking pathetically at us both.

"Of course not," we both answered.

Before she could speak, she got up and staggered to the drinks table near the window.

Should we say something? Miss Manley and I exchanged concerned looks as we heard the bottle clank against the glass as the alcohol was sloppily poured. She took a big gulp and turned around to face us, again a dramatic pose.

"It has to do with that Laura—Lulu Evans."

We just stared at her, and she lurched back to the sofa and sat down putting her head in her hands.

"Nobody knows this except Monty, and he was so furious he took the car and drove off."

We waited for more. This was agony.

She began slowly talking, looking down at the carpet. "On the night at the hotel, everybody went to the front lawn to wait out the result of whatever the fire alarm was about. There were so many people coming and going, so much excitement that I lost track of Monty. When the lights came back on in the building, I didn't see him anywhere and I had the horrible thought that he went inside to find her. Not that I didn't trust him, but you might not think it was so obvious, but I know the type of girl she was. And I've seen young women and not-so-young women throw themselves at him in order to get a head start on the stage. I either wanted to warn her off or tell Monty to steer clear."

She pulled her head up and I expected tears or remorse, but it looked more like self-pity.

"There were people in the lobby, but they were preoccupied with figuring things out and a lot of folks were coming and going. I walked past them and saw there were backstairs, and I don't know what made me do it, but I went up to the second floor, opened the door from the staircase and saw nobody about. I fully intended to go back down but something pulled me up two more flights and I figured she might be up in the attic rooms where places like that usually make the staff live. I opened the door and saw nobody around but my curiosity—damn my curiosity—made me walk down the hall and open each door as I went. Nobody was about until I got to the fifth door, and it was ajar. I pushed it open and saw Lulu, still in her performance dress, lying on her back on the floor, her torso hidden by the armchair. She was dead."

We were silent for a few moments before Miss Manley asked, "Are you sure?"

"Oh, yes. I called out her name, very softly. But it was pointless to do that. As I got closer, I was horrified to see the blood on her face and her smashed-in head. I realized whoever did this to her could be hiding in the room or still be in the building. I am such a coward! I ran all the way back down to the lawn. A few minutes later, Monty found me, berated me for going missing and insisted we go home."

"That's dreadful," I said, meaning the entire episode, not her intentions or her reaction or her suspicions about her husband, but she misunderstood and began to cry.

"I know, I know!" She took another gulp of her drink and was quiet.

"Do you really think we should keep this a secret, Christa?" Miss Manley asked in an even and soothing tone.

Christa hung her head and swayed from side to side. I thought she was trying to shake her head no, but realized she was about to pass out. I went to the sofa and pushed her back gently so she wouldn't hit her head on the coffee table, and she didn't resist at all. As I took her feet to put them up, I saw Monty's bottle of pills in the crook of the sofa.

I held up the bottle for Miss Manley to see and said, "I'll call the doctor," and sprinted to the hall telephone.

John picked up almost immediately and I briefed him, hung up the phone and returned to the sitting room to pull Christa upright, slapping her hands and pinching her arms. She groaned and grimaced but was as limp as a rag doll.

"What else can we do?" Miss Manley asked.

"Nothing much until John gets here," I said, aware I had slipped and referred to him by his given name. "We have to keep her as conscious as we can until he gets those pills out of her stomach."

John arrived quickly, didn't bother to ring the bell, crashed the unlocked door fully open and ran down the hall where I flagged him into the sitting room.

"Gastric lavage," he said, scrabbling in his bag and pulling out a tube and a suction device. "She's not going to like this, but we've got to get that stuff out. Do you know how long ago she may have taken the pills?"

I shook my head. "We've been here about twenty minutes and there's no telling how much earlier she took them. If she took any, that is."

"Better safe than sorry. Have you ever seen this procedure?"

"Yes, someone was brought into the hospital who had overdosed and a few of us were able to observe."

"Well?" he said, indicating I ought to know what was needed.

As I turned, I could hear that Christa was not entirely unconscious, which was a positive sign, and she protested as she was being positioned.

I went quickly to the kitchen asking Alice to fill a pitcher with warm water and found a bucket under the sink, grabbed several dish towels and returned to the sitting room. John nodded approval. I asked Miss Manley to find additional towels, and she left to locate a bathroom, returning with several, one that I draped around my waist just in case. John positioned Christa on her left side on the sofa and, speaking gently, explained what he was about to do to, and she whimpered in response. He took a tube from his medical bag, and slowly fed it into her mouth with care getting past the difficulty of navigating the esophagus and thus into her stomach. I was there to assist and since she protested and might move, I needed to hold her steady while Miss Manley spoke reassuringly that it would be over soon.

The first step was to aspirate what was in her stomach, not a pleasant sight, but Alice held the bucket steady, turning her head away but John and I looked to see if we could discern any intact pills. Miss Manley kept up her calm cadence while John infused about a cup of the warm water cautiously into her stomach as Christa moaned again. He aspirated again and seeing the fluid was not clear repeated the process. It was a messy, nasty job but I had assisted at more awful procedures. The fifth time produced clear liquid and the tube was slowly withdrawn, accompanied by Christa's coughing and retching though there nothing left to bring up.

John nodded to Alice, who took the bucket away, and Miss Manley patted the patient's hand. We sat her upright and John suggested instead of calling for an ambulance, which would take some time, that he drive her to the hospital in Pittsfield, a significant trip, but seated upright with the chilly air blowing in her face, it would have to do since nothing else was available.

"Christa, don't worry. Everything will be all right," Miss Manley said.

John trotted ahead to start the car while Miss Manley and I helped Christa into the hallway, out the door, down the steps, into the car, and they sped away.

"She'll probably be all right," I said to Miss Manley.

She put her hands up to her face and shook her head. "What a terrible thing to have happened."

I had other thoughts on my mind. First, was Christa telling the truth or had she killed Lulu? She told Monty what she had seen, and he conveniently left the house, leaving behind a full decanter of liquor and a bottle of pills that she could access. Or did he actually kill Lulu and left Christa to take the blame and her own life when he wasn't there? Or was the almost-overdose an accident? And what had killing Constance to do with any of these people? CR, Bernard and Catherine knew her but if they were to be believed, none but Bernard knew she was at the hotel.

I let all those questions stew in my head during the short drive home. I was hoping Miss Manley would take the task of telling Glenda what happened so I could save my energy to fix a simple dinner for us all. With that in mind, I shooed them into the sitting room and stayed in the kitchen to put it together. A half hour later, our meal of cold chicken, tomato aspic and corn pudding cooked earlier by Annie was set on the dining room table.

"What an incredible thing!" Glenda said.

I agreed and added, "What has Lulu Evans got to do with Constance Symington? The only thing I can imagine is that they met living on the fourth floor of the hotel."

"Do you think the maids and the band members fraternized?" she asked.

"I don't know. There was a common lounge area so they may have been in contact. I think I told you that I saw a locket around Constance's neck with the initials CS. Perhaps someone picked up on that and made a connection."

"That seems highly unlikely," Miss Manley said. "CS are common initials."

"You're right. Another maid said she called herself Carol so no one would have imagined that wasn't her name. What a muddle!"

Miss Manley guided our conversation to less morbid thoughts, such as what activities were planned for Stuart's arrival and the weekend. There was supposed to be a fair in Adams on Saturday; church, of course, on Sunday; and perhaps a game of tennis to fit in the busy schedule. We chatted on through dinner, only stopping when I got up to answer the telephone. It was John calling from the Pittsfield hospital to say that Christa would stay the night, that she seemed stable and a penitent Monty Davis was on his way from Highfields, having heard of what transpired after his angry departure.

"Do you think she'll be safe?" I asked, not entirely sure of Monty's intentions.

"I took the liberty of hiring a private nurse who will stay by her bedside all night. I'm sure there won't be any more incidents. But I am determined to have him get rid of those damned pills!"

Chapter 20

I had a busy morning at the Adams office, where people were in the habit of calling to make an appointment rather than just showing up at the door as they often did in West Adams. This made for a manageable scheduling of patients, but the difficulty was that each telephone call was a matter of a five-minute conversation about not just which day and what time was available but the need of the caller to explain their symptoms in more detail than was necessary. I think some of them expected me to deliver a diagnosis right then by asking what I thought the matter might be, but I certainly could not ask them additional questions as that was not my role, and I wasn't going to interrupt the doctor in the exam room for him to take such calls. A few of the individuals became annoyed with me, and that led to my explaining that I was not qualified to make a diagnosis. If this is what Dr. Mitchell had encountered or, heaven forbid, encouraged, it was no wonder he was ready for retirement.

We did have one walk-in close to noon. Montgomery Davis. I was so taken aback at seeing him after the events of the night before that I stammered a greeting and asked how Christa was before knowing I shouldn't have said that.

"I'm here to see the doctor," he said, looking around the reception area and seeming relieved at not seeing any other patients.

"The doctor is not with a patient at the moment," I said, gesturing for him to sit down and then going to John's closed office door, knocking softly before putting my head around the corner and letting him know who was outside. John raised his eyebrows and asked me to usher Monty into the room.

I had never seen the man so subdued, and I hoped that he had finally learned his lesson about leaving medication about haphazardly, considering his wife's predilection to overindulge under the strain of the events at the Mountain Aire and Lulu's body on her own front doorstep. I fully expected to hear his bombastic voice carry through the door but, to my surprise, it was all quiet murmuring for a long time. I would get the story out of John on the drive back to Adams shortly as we had afternoon appointments there.

Monty nodded politely to me when he left, just as I picked up the telephone to answer a call from Inspector Gladstone. John took up the extension in his office and I closed the door to give him privacy. What now?

I busied myself with paperwork, checking the supply closet to make sure we had enough stationery, envelopes and blank invoices for the following week. Friday already and I was looking forward to a quiet evening and relaxing weekend.

"Time to go!" John boomed from the other room.

I checked my watch. Noon already.

"We had better get something to eat before we leave," I suggested.

"There is a hot dog stand on the other side of town, if I may treat you to a local gourmet delicacy."

"That sounds delightful," I responded, knowing the nearby lunch counter favored tuna fish sandwiches on Friday and anything would be better than that.

We packed our things, locked up, turned the sign on the front door that said the doctor would return on Monday above his office telephone number in West Adams. The hot dog stand was more like a little travel trailer that someone had fitted out with a service window and a sizzling grill inside. They served nothing more than hot dogs with or without sauerkraut and a variety of condiments that could be added and bottles of soda. Luckily, there were several benches arrayed underneath maple trees near the parking area so we could sit down to have our lunch, although we watched other customers taking full brown bags back to their work site.

The weather was warm with a breeze fluttering the leaves as we ate in silence. It had been a long time since I had a meal on the go like this and it reminded me of what I missed about New York City. The soft pretzels, hot knishes, chestnuts in the winter, Italian ices in the summer, all the myriad flavors of the City. Here most of my meals had been strictly New England plain fare but I wasn't about to complain about Annie's cooking compared to a hot dog with mustard for my lunch.

Being comfortable with each other, we didn't feel the need to talk, and I wanted the silence to push him into telling me what both Monty and Gladstone had said. We had finished our brief meal and were back out on the country road when he finally turned to me.

"Aren't you dying to know what Monty said?" he chuckled.

"Not dying to know, but yes, I am curious."

He laughed. "I'm not making some statement about female curiosity or yours in particular, but this whole business has been strange and seems to be getting stranger."

Now he had my attention.

"Monty came in to thank me for attending to his wife last night and driving her to the hospital. He said they had argued earlier because she told him about seeing Lulu's body but hadn't told him earlier or anyone else, either. Although he didn't say so, I don't believe he thinks she suspected him of killing Lulu. But what he was really there to tell me was that she had got in the habit of taking his pills and he noticed that the bottle was missing and accused her of taking it. Big argument and he drove off, returning home later."

"So, he didn't administer the pills to her. And if we are to believe his version of events, he didn't accidently leave the bottle where she could find it."

"Evidently."

I mulled this over and didn't know whether to trust Monty's explanation.

"Gladstone was furious that he didn't learn of her admission about Lulu until this morning when Monty insisted Christa speak to him about it. Sobered up and with a good night's sleep in the hospital, she felt up to telling him all she knew. What is interesting is that the Pittsfield doctor who estimated the time of death as sometime around midnight was clearly wrong. She was already dead a few hours earlier."

"How did he make such an error?" I was shocked to think that we had all assumed the Big City doctor would be immune to mistakes.

"Who knows? I would hate to think he was careless in his examination. The lividity was a clue to me that someone had changed the position of the body after death. In addition, if the body were moved several times from a warm place, such as her hotel room, to a cooler place like the trunk of a car, left out in the cool evening and then moved again, it could have affected the temperature of the body and thus the estimated time of death."

"Interesting," I said, although I thought it puzzling more than anything.

We completed the ride to West Adams, each of us lost in our own thoughts and bracing for the appointments of the afternoon. It turned out to be a rather mundane end to the week and John decided to let me go home a little earlier than usual.

I rounded the edge of the back garden to Miss Manley's house and saw that her nephew, Stuart, had already arrived from the City, his yellow Packard slightly dust covered from the journey. He and Glenda were in the sitting room with Miss Manley while he told of the hazards of the trip, assisting a young woman who had a flat tire, coming across a farm stand and purchasing corn on the cob and strawberries.

"Silly!" Glenda said, tapping him on the leg in mild annoyance. "We can get all of that here, of course."

Stuart beamed at her, likely thrilled that this beautiful and forgiving creature was his wife. Had he asked, I would have agreed that he was extremely lucky.

We listened to further chat about the office, people and projects of which I had no knowledge when the doorbell rang, an unusual thing in this town except on formal occasions.

"I'll get it," Stuart said, jumping up to preempt Annie's exit from the kitchen.

"Who is it?" Glenda asked me since I had a bit of a view of the foyer from my armchair.

"Your tenant. Douglas," I whispered.

"Oh, dear," she said, getting up with a frown on her face.

There was more talking at the front door and Miss Manley gave me a quizzical look to which I shrugged. I didn't know what was going on, either. A few moments later, the door closed, and Stuart and Glenda came back to the sitting room.

"You'll never guess! Douglas has invited us for a backyard cocktail."

"That's nice," Miss Manley said.

"You're invited, too, of course," Glenda added. "And Aggie. I let him know there were additional lawn chairs in the garage."

"This is a turn of events," I said.

"He said he felt awful about what happened. With Lulu Evans, I presume, although he didn't specify."

"Maybe he has decided to stay through the fall," I suggested.

"Or maybe he can't pay the rent and is trying to soften me up," Glenda said. Since becoming a landlord, she saw the dark lining in every silver cloud.

"Don't worry, honey bun," Stuart said.

"I'm going to change," I said, and went upstairs looking forward to a bit of social activity.

***

It may only have been my take on things, but it seemed that people were being more relaxed about alcohol consumption compared to when I first arrived, although it was still done more surreptitiously in front of the hired help. Now that Douglas had extended the invitation openly, we all set about to add to the festivities with cheese and crackers, a bowl of olives and lemon slices.

Douglas stood as we approached and shook hands all around, then turned to introduce Lois, the girlfriend, who had provided a solid alibi for him. She was a willowy creature with long, tawny hair escaping from a clip intended to hold it back, wearing a diaphanous light green caftan that made it seem she floated rather than walked toward us, hand outstretched. It was a soft, almost boneless hand that shook mine and I wondered if she worked anywhere that she could be here in West Adams so often; she surely wasn't a local. Introductions completed, we sat, and I was mesmerized by the breeze moving Lois's long outfit as if it were a rippling brook. I tried hard to recall whether the young woman I had seen in Douglas' lap was Lois, but now I couldn't be sure.

Stuart asked Lois if she were of The Lancaster family, and she smiled coyly before shaking her head. Her lack of pedigree did not dissuade him from asking her questions that were intended to elicit her connections and I was a little affronted that he never subjected me to the same interrogations: was I related to The Burnsides, for example. It was probably because Glenda had told him so much about me before I met him that he knew all there was to know. Good old reliable, dependable Aggie. I realized the caftan was lovely but absurdly exotic here in West Adams and would likely look like a nightgown on me.

Douglas produced a seltzer bottle to Glenda's immense pleasure as if she had never seen one before and she insisted on a generous spritz into her glass of gin. What a happy group we suddenly were, the notion that someone had dumped a body on Douglas' doorstep not too long ago, which he in turn had positioned in front of Monty Davis' door, was forgotten in the brittle chatter of the urbane group.

As usual, Stuart dominated the conversation, telling Douglas and Lois about his publishing business, the many books he had written and the direction he intended to take the company. Of course, Douglas's ears perked up at what seemed an invitation to expound upon his scripts, a novel he was working on and soon they were in an earnest discussion of how a possible collaboration could take place. I could see a small frown starting on Glenda's face as she anticipated another investment scheme on the horizon.

During a lull in their conversation, I brought up the fact that Cash Ridley was staying at the Mountain Aire and perhaps he might be interested in investing in a play. The eyebrows of both men shot up at the possibility of an investor of that caliber as everyone in New York, as Stuart would say, knew of Cash Ridley.

He shot me a wounded look, wondering how I knew the man and why I had not previously shared the connection.

I answered his look with, "Stuart, you weren't here long enough to make the acquaintance last weekend."

"And I thought the Mountain Aire was such a poky little place," he said.

"It's a lovely place," Miss Manley offered.

I think she was about to qualify that statement by mentioning the recent fatal events connected with it but then remembered Douglas's association and looked back down at her half-filled glass.

"The Fosters could do so much more with it," Stuart continued.

"They have. In fact, the rumor is that Cash Ridley is in the process of buying it," I said.

The two men nearly jumped out of their chairs. There was indeed a gold mine nearby and by the looks they gave each other, it appeared they meant to follow up somehow and develop a scheme to access it before Ridley's money was foolishly wasted on some other venture.

As they engaged in a lively conversation, I attempted to talk to Lois, who had a distant, distracted air about her as though speaking to us mere mortals was like attempting a foreign language. However, once I mentioned that I was from New York and had lived in the City before moving up here for work, she warmed up to the notion that I might not be a hayseed after all.

The party was interrupted by a car screeching to a halt in the Lewises' driveway and the sound of a particularly silly song sung by Roger:

"Sarasponda, Sarasponda, Sarasponda, Sarasponda,
Rett Sett Sett.
Adorayo! Adoray boomday oh!"

Meanwhile, Bobby accompanied him with a bass line, "Boomda! Boomda! Boomda!"

We stared before bursting into laughter at their exuberance and their ignorance of being overheard. But once they came into view and saw us, they stopped abruptly and joined in the hilarity with a few more "Boomdas."

"Hullo, everyone!" Roger shouted merrily. He wasn't that much younger than I, but somehow, I considered him the epitome of youth: raucous, healthy, his face tan and his hair blonde from his work on the tennis courts.

"Come sit down, my good gentlemen," Stuart said loudly to them. As there was an obvious drinking party going on, they were more than happy to oblige, sitting on the grass as all but one of the chairs were occupied. Stuart knew Roger from previous visits, but Bobby was a new face to him as Lois was to the two young men. They smiled and introduced themselves but clearly were mystified by this ethereal woman in her flowing outfit who had the air of daydreaming even when speaking directly to you.

"Gosh, I'm certainly glad that you beat the rap," Roger blurted to Douglas who took the comment in stride.

"Yes, terrible business, and I'm glad it is all behind me."

"Miss Burnside, did you tell them about the woman at the hotel in the laundry basket?"

I couldn't believe he brought that up and was embarrassed to see that Stuart thought this was going to be some amusing story that I had yet to tell. I disabused him immediately.

"No, Roger, I did not. But many of you have heard that someone was found strangled at the hotel and it was determined that she was the estranged wife of Cash Ridley's assistant."

"And Cash Ridley's daughter!" Roger added.

Everyone was quiet and I noticed that Lois's eyes widened.

"That's enough," Miss Manley said sternly. "I object to any kind of macabre interest in the misfortunes of others."

"Well said, Auntie," Stuart added sententiously.

After a few moments, he couldn't help but pick up the thread of the conversation.

"Do you think it is somehow connected to the death of that young girl?"

Most of us wished to move away from the discussion entirely, but Bobby piped up with his own theory.

"Don't you think it is odd that it has been two women? Both connected to the Mountain Aire? My mother had a fit about me continuing to work there even if it is only a desk job."

"Excuse me," Miss Manley said abruptly and walked to her own house.

I wondered if any of us should accompany her, but neither Stuart nor Glenda made a move to go after her. Clearly, they wanted to continue the analysis. As did I.

"The manner of killing was a blow to the head for Lulu and strangulation for Constance," I said. "It speaks to a man or a strong woman effecting the deed, perhaps caught by surprise and reacting in fear and having no other weapon."

They stared at me open-mouthed. I was a bit surprised by my bold comments.

"But why?" Lois asked.

"Yes, what did they have in common except they both worked at the hotel?" Glenda asked.

"Their rooms were on the same floor. There is a communal women's washroom—perhaps they had occasion to chat at some point."

"Maybe Lulu told the other woman something that she shouldn't have!" Bobby concluded.

"That's a good point," Stuart said.

"About what? Something about Cash Ridley? After all, Lulu didn't know that the maid who called herself Carol was actually his daughter."

"It may have been something about money," Glenda suggested. "Such as Lulu talking about Cash Ridley buying the hotel and then what would his daughter do? She'd be found out."

"Maybe Lulu was boasting about how CR was going to bankroll her singing career," Roger suggested. Where he had picked up on the nickname or the jargon, I couldn't imagine. Perhaps he had been hanging out with the band members and absorbed some of the slang.

"Gosh, I'm thirsty," he said bluntly. "What's a guy have to do to get a drink?"

It was a bold statement but made with a broad smile and Douglas relented and poured each of the young men a smaller portion than he had administered to us. Even that was obviously appreciated and loosened tongues even more.

"Here's my theory," Roger began. "Cash Ridley is such a big shot that he's probably made lots of enemies. That's why he's hiding out in the Berkshires, until things cool down in the City."

"I think you've been watching too many gangster movies," I said.

"No, really. Think about it. Don't you think it strange that he's holed up at the hotel and then gets sweet on a songbird? What do we know about Lulu Evans? Maybe she is some guy's moll and she was playing CR for a stiff."

"Where did you pick up such language?" Nina said, coming up suddenly from the parsonage.

"Oh, hello, Aunt Nina," Roger said, properly admonished.

She looked from him and his glass to Douglas who merely shrugged.

"It's a watered-down drink," Roger said in his defense.

"In that case, please get me a chair and I would be pleased to have one as well. Stuart, how is business going?"

This change of topic allowed him to go on at length about his 'imprint' as he referred to it and the many projects he would attempt in the coming months.

"Maybe we ought to help your aunt with dinner?" Glenda asked him.

"Annie's here tonight," he answered, somewhat annoyed at the interruption of thought.

"If you're looking for investment opportunities, why not approach Cash Ridley? He seemed to have wanted to invest in Lulu Evans's career. Maybe he would want to be known as the empresario who brought the playwright Douglas Martin to Broadway." I said it tongue in cheek but both he and Stuart looked at each other and then at me.

"You're brilliant!" Stuart said. "When can you make the introduction?"

Chapter 21

What had I got myself into? Now Stuart was going to hound me for the remainder of the weekend to set up a meeting that would be nothing short of awkward. CR knew me as a nurse and as a dinner companion to John Taylor. How in the world could I casually introduce him to Stuart, who would bombard him with his preposterous proposals of adventure novels for adults being sold to young boys? Or some hare-brained collaboration with a playwright whose works he had probably never heard of? I felt no obligation whatsoever to enable that introduction and tried all through dinner that night to change the subject to something more neutral but whenever I did, Stuart would begin laying compliments on me: what an intuitive mind I had, how lucky West Adams was to have me there, etc. Even Miss Manley and Glenda were getting annoyed by his obvious courting technique.

"Stuart, please stop pestering me about it. There is no reason why you can't go to the Mountain Aire and make an appointment with him."

"That's not how business is done. I need an entree."

"I sighed in frustration. Tomorrow is Saturday and there is no reason why we couldn't go to the hotel and have tea or something. There is every probability we might run into him and then I'll make an introduction. Not any other way."

"Brava!" he crowed.

When we took the dishes into the kitchen, Glenda whispered, "Thank you."

"I don't know why you should thank me about his screwball idea."

"Because he'll pitch it and inflate the investment amount needed. When Mr. Ridley refuses, Stuart will realize we don't have that amount ourselves to fund it. Nor does Douglas, I shouldn't think. He'll have to drop it."

I looked at her with new admiration. She had Stuart pegged, all right, and had figured out a way to outfox him without seeming to stand in his way.

***

The next morning our little caravan set out for the Mountain Aire. John and I in his car to check up on CR, Douglas and Lois in his car, and Glenda, Stuart and Miss Manley in the third automobile.

"I intend to make my examination of CR before those two men raise his blood pressure with any scatterbrained investment opportunity," John said.

"I know I said I wouldn't force an introduction, but perhaps it wouldn't be too out of line to suggest that there were two men waiting to meet Cash, having heard of his presence in the hotel." I winced as I said it and could feel John's eyes on me.

"That's up to you," he said mildly.

"We just have to make sure that Glenda and Miss Manley are occupied doing something else. The men can't very well make a business pitch with all of us hovering around. Oh, I wish I hadn't agreed to this. I can't think of a more unpleasant way to spend a Saturday morning."

"Oh, I can," he smiled at me. "Because we're going to be meeting up with Inspector Gladstone."

I held my head in mock pain just to make him laugh.

Saturdays at the hotel were busy with new guests checking in and day trippers stopping by to admire the views, consume a meal, and possibly satisfy their ghoulish interest in the two murders recently associated with the location.

John and I went up to the third floor while the rest of our group sauntered out to the terrace to admire the view and make themselves comfortable for the upcoming 'accidental' meeting. CR was looking very well, I thought; his color was good, he may have lost a few pounds and he had the wisdom not to smoke. At least not while we were there. He and the doctor went into the adjacent bedroom while I went over to the desk where Catherine shuffled through some papers.

"Working on a Saturday!" I said, fully aware that I was, too.

"No rest for the wicked, eh?" She smiled and added, "I never mentioned how I enjoyed tennis in spite of how the afternoon ended."

"Yes, that was terrible. Tell me, how is CR taking it?"

"It's the second blow in such a short time. I think despite his great affection for this part of the world, he will probably pick up sticks soon."

"I'm sorry to hear that. So soon after purchasing the hotel, too."

"No, that deal is off. I don't think the Fosters are all that disappointed, to tell the truth. They may feel that all these recent tragedies have harmed their reputation, but regular visitors recognize that these things happen and are not the fault of the owners. Sorry to say that it might actually improve business."

I was surprised by her cool assessment of the situation but that was probably why she was successful in her position, able to accommodate herself to whatever was thrown her way. It was a characteristic that I had begun to appreciate.

She motioned me to sit down while she finished tidying her desk and we chatted about the possibility of another tennis date in the next week. The door to the bedroom opened and John exited, not saying anything. A few moments later he was joined by CR who was smiling ear to ear.

"In the peak of health!" he announced.

John's small, satisfied grin indicated this was not hyperbole. I was pleased that whatever emotional trauma he had suffered, his vital signs were not in jeopardy.

"Let's go down to the terrace and have some coffee," CR suggested. John and I exchanged glances, anticipating the possibly awkward scene ahead.

"I'll stay here, if you don't mind," Catherine said.

The positive results of the exam had CR in an ebullient mood, and he talked loudly all the way down to the lobby about how well he felt and the plans he had for going back to the City soon, going sailing with some business associates, taking a train trip up to Montreal. When in a good mood, it seemed he talked incessantly, perhaps another reason Catherine sought some time to herself.

We walked out to the terrace and Glenda caught my eye, waving for us to come to their table. CR's eyes lit up at the sight of the pretty young woman he recognized, and he made a beeline to where the group sat under a canvas umbrella.

Introductions were made among those who weren't acquainted, and CR surprised most of us by jumping right into asking what Stuart did for a living. We hadn't expected this to occur so soon, and we looked at each other, wondering whether we ought to get up right then—a strange thing to do—and let their conversation take its course or wait for a more natural way to make our exit.

"An author? What books have you written?" CR asked.

When Stuart mentioned the first book in his series, CR nearly exploded with enthusiasm.

"I've read your books! *The Peril of Dunbar*. What a fantastic story! I've been to Scotland, and you captured the atmosphere, the grey stone buildings, the damp, the quiet suspicion of the locals. The rain!" He slapped his leg as he laughed at the memory.

Stuart seemed to have grown six inches in height from the accolade and he prompted CR with the title of another book, resulting in a cascade of compliments and recollections of the escapades of the hero as he escaped the dastardly villains yet again.

CR realized he had left Douglas out of the conversation and politely asked him about his profession. When he answered, I thought CR would fly out of his chair.

"A playwright? That's fantastic. I wonder if I've seen any of your works?"

This went on for some time with no one else able to get a word into the conversation until John broke in.

"I'm sorry to interrupt this lively conversation, but Nurse Burnside and I are due to meet someone shortly. But please, go on without us." He held up his hands in apology, stood, pulled out my chair and we made our way to the lobby.

"That was extraordinary!" I said.

John shook his head. "I guess there is no accounting for taste. Well, if Cash Ridley loves them and wants to invest in Stuart's company, more power to him."

"Thank you for rescuing us from the mutual admiration society meeting. But are we going home now?" I asked.

"I told you about Inspector Gladstone. Ah, there he is!"

And there he was, sitting patiently in an armchair in the lobby with his hat still on his head and not looking too pleased to be there. We joined him and he and John got right down to the matter at hand.

"We've looked in Lulu Evans' room and Constance Symington's room and have not found anything to help with this investigation."

"Has anyone been in the rooms to clean or retrieve clothing or jewelry?" John asked.

"No. They were left as we found them, and they are now locked."

John looked at me and back at the inspector.

"Why don't we take one more look. I have a feeling we'll find something that will help."

And with Gladstone's slight grunt of annoyance the three of us made our way to the elevator to the fourth floor.

Chapter 22

Compared to the activity in the lobby and on the terrace, the fourth floor was eerily quiet, perhaps because the maids were preparing rooms downstairs and the band members resting up for the performance in the evening.

Inspector Gladstone unlocked the door to Lulu Evans's room where we were met with the scent of stale perfume in the dark and airless space.

"May I open a window?" John asked the inspector, who nodded. The shade was pulled up, the sash thrown open and the inspector turned on the overhead light. It didn't improve the look of the place.

The room was a shambles. The bed was unmade, there were clothes on the bedspread, shoes strewn across the floor and clothes hanging out of the drawers of the chest. The low-slung vanity was covered by a hairbrush and bobby pins, several lipstick tubes, eye pencils, a rectangular mascara box, still open with the brush on its side, rouge, a powder puff, and a dusting of powder on the edge of a drawer.

"Is this what it looked like when you found it?" I asked, used to living in spartan and tidy circumstances. Unfortunately, the inspector took my comment the wrong way.

"Yes, I am sorry to say. My men had a terrible time trying not to disturb that which was already a disturbed scene." He glowered at me.

"I apologize. I can't imagine she left her room like this. And if she didn't, then who did riffle through everything?"

"Good question. Her cousin saw the room and didn't bat an eyelash. Evidently, it was her habit to live like this and one of the reasons that they didn't share a room."

"May we look around?" John asked and got approval from Gladstone.

I went to the small desk in the corner of the room by stepping gingerly over a satin pump and opened the one drawer which held only a few sheets of hotel stationary, envelopes and a postcard. Its main function seemed to have been another place for Lulu to park an evening bag and a tangle of stockings. Touching such an intimate item of clothing was sad and humbling and I quickly closed the drawer.

Gladstone stood by the door while we poked, prodded and lifted things by turn and didn't come across anything other than a messy room.

"I guess you've looked under the mattress," I said. My comment was met with a withering look from the inspector.

I managed a contrite smile.

"Care to see the other room now?" he asked.

John shut the window and we followed the inspector down the hall to what had been Constance's room. It was a smaller version of the rooms we had seen on that floor due to the angle of the roofline giving it a claustrophobic feeling. In contrast to Lulu's room that looked like a bomb had exploded, Constance's room appeared not to have been lived in at all. The bed was made with hospital corners, the few items of clothing in the closet were hung precisely, the drawers held neatly folded underwear, a slip and carefully rolled stockings. The vanity had an expensive hairbrush with a comb placed crosswise in the bristles, a lipstick and a packet of hairnets. It was as if she had just arrived and didn't plan on staying long.

John stood by the door and scratched his head while I looked out the little window that had a view of the parking lot and the mountains behind.

"Do you think she could have seen something from up here?" I asked.

The inspector and John crowded over to the window to look down.

"Not much to see," Gladstone said.

"Cars. People. Coming and going," I said.

He looked at me.

"Could we go back to Lulu's room?" John asked.

Gladstone agreed with an exasperated exhalation.

When we entered Lulu's room again John walked to the vanity and put his hand out to the spilt powder.

"That's not face powder. That's rosin."

"Oh, no!" I said. "Not Lester!" I had really warmed to the man.

"What are you talking about?" Gladstone asked. "Rosin is used by baseball pitchers."

Now I was confused.

John explained. "Yes, pitchers use rosin bags to keep their hands dry. So do gymnasts. But this may have come from a rosin stick that musicians use on their bow strings. As a bassist might."

"Let's see if Lester is in his room," Gladstone said.

He might have been resting in anticipation of the evening's performance since his hair was on end and he blinked at us when he opened his door,

"What can you tell me about Lulu Evans that you haven't yet disclosed?" Gladstone said after we had entered the room.

"What? Nothing." He seemed genuinely surprised.

His modest room seemed even smaller with three more people inside and the bass standing guard in the corner.

"Don't you have a case for that?" John asked.

"I did. But it's been missing since the night of the blackout or fire alarm or whatever happened. We all left the building quickly thinking the worst and, of course, I took her with me. The case was in my room, or so I thought, but with all the people coming and going from the building anyone could have come in and taken it. Not much use to anyone but a fellow musician but the brotherhood is strong in that respect."

"Can you prove it was taken that night?"

"Well, I sure complained about it after the hubbub calmed down and we were allowed back in the building. She's awkward to carry without the bag."

Gladstone stared at Lester hoping for a breakthrough, but the big man just put his fingers to his head to smooth his hair. He seemed as perplexed as we were.

"Don't go anywhere," the inspector warned him.

"How could I? I don't have a car." Lester said.

We took the elevator back to the lobby and his last comment stuck in my head.

"Can we sit down for a moment?" I asked.

We found a quiet corner and it looked like Gladstone was happy to be off his feet.

"What we know is that poor Lulu was moved around a bit after she died. The lividity on the body points to that. According to Christa, she was killed here." John asked.

"What if she were killed here and transported out in Lester's bass bag? It's the perfect size for the task," I said. Both men looked at me as if I had actually considered doing it myself.

"She had to be taken out of the building and away from here by car and none of the musicians has a car."

"Except Harry Williams," Gladstone said. "The man with the hair trigger temper, so I'm told." He stood and stomped off towards the ballroom. One look between John and me said we had come this far, so let's continue. We trotted to keep up with the inspector, who stormed into the ballroom interrupting a jazzy riff that Harry was playing on the piano. He looked up as the three of us approached with fear in his eyes that was mitigated by a broad smile.

"Do you have a car?" Gladstone asked.

"Yes," he answered.

"Let's go see it."

"Right now?"

Gladstone's lack of an answer was answer enough. Harry got up and smiled again at all of us and began some distracting chatter.

"We're expecting a crowd tonight, I tell you. Sophia is not quite in full voice yet, but she soon will be."

"Don't overtax her or it will take that much longer for her to recover fully," John said.

"We had a conversation about her just talking through the lyrics on a song. Could sound really sexy that way."

It seemed an inappropriate remark to me, but I supposed musicians were more earthy than us regular folks. He twirled the car keys in his fingers as we made our way to his car parked across the lot from the door that led out from the ballroom and the nearby back stairwell.

"Here she is," he said proudly.

It was a Ford Model A station wagon with wood inlay on the sides. With all the instruments and the band members, he needed a large vehicle.

"Could you please unlock it?" Gladstone asked.

"Sure thing. He put the key in the lock, opened the door and held out his hand to show there was nothing to see. He closed the door, opened the back door, made the same motion then tilted the seat forward so the back seat could be examined.

Gladstone went over to the passenger side with John and me following while Harry unlocked it, motioning with his hand that there was nothing worth seeing. "I'm not transporting illegal booze, if that's what you think," he said with a laugh.

"Now, please open the back."

We followed while Harry unlocked it. He swung it wide open and stood with his hands on his hips. "See, no booze." He lifted the canvas bass case out to show that the trunk was otherwise empty except for a tire iron and some rags.

"What's that?" Gladstone pointed to the object in his hand.

"Lester's case. He asked me to store it for him."

"That's not what he told us," I said.

There was a moment of silence as Harry realized that we knew more than we were saying.

"Here," he said and pushed the case onto Gladstone so hard that it hurtled him into John and me, knocking all three of us backwards towards the curbing of the parking lot. Harry jumped in the car, started it quickly and tore away down the road.

We were astonished enough not to say anything but picked ourselves off the ground while Gladstone sat with the canvas bag in his hands. He unzipped it and looked inside to see a dusting of rosin which he rubbed between his fingers.

"Gotcha!" he declared.

"But…" I started to say, pointing at the station wagon receding in the distance.

"If he continues at that speed, he'll either crash or get a ticket. If not, with that distinctive an automobile, we'll have him in custody by the morning."

Chapter 23

Gladstone was right about one thing. There wasn't a crash, and he didn't get a speeding ticket, but Harry was spotted trying to look inconspicuous stopping in Beckett for gas. The owner was about to shut down for the day and he just didn't like the cut of his jib, as he related to Gladstone later. While Harry used the restroom, the owner did not fill up the car with gas but confiscated the car keys, locked the door to the station and called the police.

We knew Harry had a temper, but no one expected him to break the front windows of the gas station either in rage or an attempt to break out to get his keys back. He finally gave up and waited for Officer Reed to pick him up.

We heard the details the next day from Officer Reed who, now as a guest of honor, took his tea in the sitting room with Miss Manley, Glenda, Stuart, John and me, with Annie standing proudly by his chair.

"What did he have to say for himself?" John asked.

"Just as you may have supposed: between the sets—that's what the musicians call the group of numbers that they play—he went to confront Lulu about her conversations with Monty Davis and Cash Ridley."

"Remember," I interjected, "they were both vying for her attention or a contract with her. There were some heated words as Monty thought she could be his next Broadway star while CR was going to bankroll her in New York nightclub act."

"That meant that she would be leaving the band," John said.

"Yes, and she was what made the Harry Williams Band so special. He followed her to her room and confronted her, they had an argument and in a fit of passion, he smashed his fist into her temple."

The women in the room gasped at his words.

"Harry said he was appalled at what he had done. And very sorry, too, but I don't know about that," Officer Reed said. "After he killed her, he went out into the hall, pulled the fire alarm to create a distraction, went into Lester's nearby room, grabbed the bass case thinking to put her into it. Somehow, he never saw Christa come upstairs and she didn't see him. He returned to Lulu's room, stuffed her in the case and then put her in the trunk of his car. He came back to the front lawn and mingled with the guests and band members long enough to be noticed, then went back to his car and took the back road from the hotel. He didn't know where he was going and didn't really know the area very well but drove until he came here to West Adams."

Miss Manley shook her head.

"He said he saw the lights were off in some of the houses and he chose one, unzipped the case, put Lulu on the doorstep and drove away."

"You mean he didn't intentionally put it at a particular house?"

"From what he said, he didn't know the area at all. It was just by chance."

"Lucky me," Glenda said. Stuart patted her hand.

"Sometime later, Douglas and his girlfriend, who may have been drinking." Here I paused for emphasis, "came back home and had the fright of their lives seeing a bloody body on the doorstep. Any rational person would have called the police, but he felt everyone was so antagonistic toward him and his bohemian lifestyle, he decided the best course of action was to put her somewhere else. And where else but at Monty Davis's door. The man who had spurned his artistic ambitions."

"Exactly," Officer Reed said.

"That's why you found rosin in Lulu's hair—from the case in which she was transported—and petals from Glenda's rosebush where she was first placed."

"Yes, that's it!"

We were quiet for a few moments.

"Charlie, that was brilliant," Annie said to Officer Reed, who colored pleasantly under her compliments.

"But what about Constance Symington?" Miss Manley asked. "Who killed her?"

"People were concerned about her connection to CR and their estrangement, her lack of a final divorce from her husband and what her intentions were in being at the Mountain Aire. But I think she was just in the wrong place at the wrong time."

"That's exactly right," Officer Reed said. "She must have heard the argument from all the way down the hall and then a period of silence. She saw Harry taking a cumbersome object down the back stairs and only later put it together that it must have been Lulu's body. She confronted Harry about it and, well, although he denies it, we know the rest."

***

It was a somber ending to a Saturday evening as I thought about poor Lulu, so young, ambitious and talented and oblivious to the chaos she caused in more than one man's life and one man's deranged mind. My heart went out to Constance, whom I didn't even know, who was possibly hoping to openly reconcile with her husband before meeting such a nasty end.

As Roger informed us, there was obviously no performance at the Mountain Aire that evening and the band members had packed up and gotten someone to take them to Pittsfield to catch a bus to Manhattan. I hoped they would find employment in these difficult times. Sofia was staying on for a bit to deal with Lulu's meager possessions and see that she got a proper burial. Roger also told us that Cash Ridley and his staff were dismantling their office, ready to move on to the next watering hole for the remainder of the summer. Monty and Christa, absolved of any involvement in the murders, would probably keep a low profile until their lease ran out.

The next day was Sunday and I looked forward to attending church with Miss Manley as a way to sweep aside the lingering feelings of sadness and loss that I felt for two women whom I didn't know very well. Reverend Lewis gave a lovely sermon about the value of life, no matter how long or short, and I felt myself crying softly before being patted on the hand by Miss Manley.

Stuart and Glenda left shortly after Sunday dinner, both subdued by the events of the past days despite his new alliance with Douglas and CR that I hope worked out well for their sakes. I poked around in the garden in the afternoon, wrote a letter home without mentioning the murders, which would horrify my parents and make them pressure me to return home. As evening closed in, John came by and asked me to go to his house for a bit of star gazing. It was a puzzling request, but I agreed, and on the way, I asked him why it was he didn't attend church in town.

"Don't get me wrong, I like Reverend Lewis and respect his work. Organized religion is just not for me."

He directed me to two chaises longues in his back garden that he had tilted back so we could see the sky without craning our necks.

"I tend to think of this as my church. Perseids."

I looked at him inquiringly.

"I misspoke when I said star gazing. We're looking at the Perseid meteor shower that happens this time every year. See?"

I looked up and shortly saw a shooting star arc from one part of the sky to the other.

"That's wonderful! Look, there's another! How is it I have never noticed them before?"

"Nose to the grindstone, that's why," he said, touching the tip of my nose.

"No, really?"

"I suspect it's because you're a city girl and the streetlights tend to reduce the dark sky as they are intended to."

We watched in silence for a few more minutes before he spoke again.

"How are things in New York?"

"My parents are well, thank you. My brother's getting ready to leave for college.

"No, I meant the position at the hospital."

"Oh, that." I was quiet for a few moments. "I haven't really pursued it further."

"That's good. I mean, I guess that means that you'll be staying on here."

"Yes, I've really come to love it here. I'll stay until Thanksgiving."

He was speechless for a moment.

"And then?"

"Well, we'll have to go to Pelham for the holiday so you can meet my parents."

John smiled and pointed upward. "Look, I think I just saw my lucky star."

***

What happens when Aggie and John are invited for a holiday weekend by an eccentric author who knows someone is out to get her?

Christmas Recipe for Murder

Available November 2021

Check out my website and newsletter for information
on new releases:

www.Andreas-books.com

Printed in Great Britain
by Amazon

34680371R00096